The F...

DETECTIVE

DOVE

Zuni Blue

Amaria & Sariel

LONDON

THE FAT GIRL WHO NEVER EATS

For more information, please contact:

Zuni Blue at www.zuniblue.com

Print ISBN: 978-1097691203

First Edition August 2013

This Edition May 2019

100 Free Gifts For You

There are 100 FREE printables waiting for you!

Certificates, bookmarks, wallpapers and more! You can choose your favourite colour: red, yellow, pink, green, orange, purple or blue.

You don't need money or an email address. Check out www.zuniblue.com to print your free gifts today.

CONTENTS

Case File No.5

In London, England, you'll find Detective Inspector Mya Dove. With four years' experience on the police force, this eight-year-old is on her way to being the best police officer ever.

Yes. The best. Her mum said so.

To inspire other kids, she's sharing case files. Case No.5: The Fat Girl Who Never Eats.

Chapter 1

Our teacher Mrs Cherry burst into class carrying a massive, green recycling bag. Inside were lots of baked bean cans, glass bottles, torn clothes and old shoes.

"Class, guess what we're doing this afternoon?" Mrs Cherry asked, her sweaty face as red as her hair. "Come on! Try to guess..."

Angel White put her hand up. She gave a mean look to anyone who dared put theirs up too.

"Yes, Angel?" Mrs Cherry said.

"Miss, are we going to create amazing artwork to sell online?" She turned back and glared at me with her blue eyes. "Some people are poor. They need the money."

She was still angry about the week I stayed at her house. We flooded her bedroom by accident and her parents were furious! They cut her allowance from ten pounds a day to one.

My allowance was five pounds a month, and only if I did my chores. Otherwise, I got nothing.

"No, Angel, we're not creating artwork," Mrs Cherry said, her bushy eyebrows twitching. "Would anyone else like to guess what we'll be doing?"

If it wasn't arts and crafts, nobody really cared.

"Recycling again!" Mrs Cherry cried. "Last time, we focused on recycling plastic.

This time, we'll focus on recycling glass, metal, clothes, shoes, and more…"

Everyone else groaned but I was excited! I'd heard about recycling glass and metal, but never knew about recycling old clothes and shoes.

I was also excited about getting another case. It was Monday afternoon and my secret boss hadn't given me one yet. What was taking so long?

"Psst!"

That was my best friend Libby, a very quiet, black girl with fluffy afro hair like mine. She waved me over, so I leaned in when Mrs Cherry wasn't looking.

"I have very important news about your secret boss," Libby whispered. "She's at home, sick with the measles."

I couldn't go and see her because I didn't know who she was or where she lived. That's why I called her my secret boss.

"Libby, did you see my secret boss's face?" I whispered. "What's she look like? What's her name?"

"Someone else gave me the note, not your boss," she said, handing me a folded piece of paper. "I can't say any more than that or I'll be in serious trouble!"

When Mrs Cherry wasn't looking, I slowly unfolded the note. I placed it on top of my notebook and rested the tip of my pencil on the page. It looked like I was writing, but really I was reading the note. Here's what it said:

Detective Inspector Mya Dove,

Unfortunately, I caught the measles from my older

brother. He did it on purpose when he hugged me last week, but I can't prove it...yet.

Anyway, that's not why I'm writing to you. There's something much worse than the measles going on!

Last week, there weren't enough burgers in the lunch hall. The dinner ladies said it was their fault for not ordering ten more, but my friends say they're lying.

I heard that the dinner ladies

DID order enough burgers, but someone ate them. Yes. The ten extra burgers were eaten by ONE person, but who?

Shelly Walters is our suspect. She's really, really fat, and everyone knows fat people eat all the food. There are other fat people at school, but Shelly is the fattest, so she has to be the burger thief.

If we know Shelly's the burger thief, just give her detention, right? Wrong! We can't without proof that she stole the burgers! Proof will be hard to find because Shelly doesn't eat anything at lunchtime. She just drinks water...

Your mission? Prove that Shelly is eating too much. We can't have students starving because of her. It's not fair!

Your reward? A bag of white grapes. They're fresh. Juicy. Tasty.

Remember to bin this note. This info can't leak out.

I'll speak to you in the toilets on Friday afternoon. Do not be late!

Don't let us down, Detective Dove. If Shelly gets away with this, there'll be ten very hungry students every lunchtime until she leaves primary school.

Once again, don't be late on Friday!

See you soon,

Your Boss

I was happy that I had another case, but…it was such an *easy* case. All I had to do was get proof that Shelly ate lots of food. That would be easy because she was so fat! I always saw fat people eating food.

Don't jump to conclusions, I thought. Whenever I do that, I get things wrong.

If an officer is wrong too many times, they're told off by their boss. I'd gotten my last few cases wrong. No wonder I hadn't been paid any grapes yet! The Children's Police Force didn't think I was doing a good job.

I had to be right this time. I had to be!

To start the case, I needed to know more about Shelly Walters, the fat girl who never eats. Who could tell me more about her?

My friend Jimmy! He had info on everyone at school. He could tell me more about Shelly. Then I'd stop her from stealing more juicy burgers.

This case should be easy, I thought, but I've said that before and been wrong.

Will I be wrong again?

Chapter 2

At breaktime, the best place to find my friend Jimmy was on the football pitch. He was the best striker, defender and goalie.

"Jimmy will know all about Shelly Walters," I said to myself. "He might even have proof that she's stealing burgers."

Jimmy was easy to spot on the football field. He was the only one not huffing and puffing. The others were all pink and sweaty.

Just outside the pitch were lots of boys and girls cheering the teams on. I would've stayed to watch, but I had a case to solve first.

"Time out," Jimmy yelled and jogged over to me. Football doesn't have time outs like basketball, but no one argued with him. They all really needed a few minutes' break.

"Hi, Mya." Jimmy pointed at the climbing frame. "Let's talk about that science project thing for Mrs Cherry."

He winked. I winked back.

There wasn't really a science project, but we had to keep the police case a secret. If we blabbed about it, Shelly would know she was under investigation for burger stealing!

Jimmy and I rushed to the climbing frame and huddled underneath. We waited a few minutes, just in case someone was listening, and then Jimmy spoke quietly.

"Mya, I've been asking around about Shelly Walters."

"What'd you find out?" I asked.

He held out his hand, so I gave him one

pound. It was a lot of money, but I really needed some info. I wanted to solve the case ASAP so I could get my green grapes.

"Shelly is in Year Two," he said, "so she's six or seven years old."

"Six or seven? Which one?"

"Dunno." He stopped to scratch one of his pink spots. They were all over his white face. "She's size...bigger than you. She's smaller than my mum when she's pregnant."

"That's not very spec...spec..."

"Specific. I know." He smoothed down his messy, brown hair. "I did my best."

"Okay, then. What does Shelly look like?" I asked.

"Blonde hair like Angel White's. White skin like mine. Hazel eyes. Very, very fat. Stays by herself a lot. No friends."

"...Is that all you know?" I crossed my arms and gave him my angriest face. "Jimmy,

I paid you one whole pound!"

"Your secret boss should reimburse you for all business expenses. Or you could claim it back on your taxes come January."

"Taxes? Business expenses? Jimmy, I don't even know what reimburse means!"

"Me neither, but that's what the accountant told my dad last week."

"I want a refund," I snapped.

"Look, I did the best I could," he said. "I asked around but no one really knows about Shelly. She stays by herself, so I can't find anything on her."

"But you know about *everyone* at school!"

"I hear gossip about people by talking to students in their class," he said. "Shelly stays by herself, so no one has anything to say about her."

"Come on, Jimmy! You didn't find out anything else?"

"Nope, but when I heard Shelly's name, I remembered something important…"

"What?" I asked.

"The burgers were stolen after Nurse Mona spoke to some students."

"What did they talk about?"

"It's a big secret," he said. "The teachers and nurses won't tell. The students won't tell either. I tried paying them, offered them sweets—"

"Did you try offering grapes? They're better than sweets."

"Mya, nobody but you loves grapes." He laughed, but I didn't find it funny.

Grapes are sweeter than any sweet. And they don't make your teeth fall out. I know baby teeth are replaced, but adult teeth aren't.

"Did Shelly see the nurse?" I asked.

Jimmy nodded.

"Who else did Nurse Mona speak to?"

Jimmy pointed at four different kids in the playground.

The first kid was a fat Asian girl with waist-length hair. She was playing with bugs and slugs by the bushes.

The second kid was a fat black boy cheering on the basketball teams. He threw his arms in the air and ran around every time someone scored.

The third kid was a fat white girl sitting on a bench with her friends. They were chatting over their mobile phones. We weren't allowed phones at school, but some people sneaked them in.

The last kid was a fat white boy watching us from the school gates. When I looked in his eyes, they narrowed and he frowned at me.

What's his problem? I thought. I haven't

done anything to him, have I?

"Jimmy, have you noticed something?" I asked. "Nurse Mona only spoke to fat kids."

They were all fat, so any of them could've been the burger thief. To find out if Shelly was the one stealing burgers, we had to investigate the other fat kids. If they weren't guilty, we'd focus on Shelly again.

"Which kid should we speak to first?" Jimmy asked.

"Let's talk to the black boy watching basketball."

"I know him," Jimmy said. "He's Daniel. Let me do the talking."

Jimmy and I went to Daniel, who was standing on the edge of the basketball court. Daniel gripped his big belly and gritted his teeth, his brown eyes fixed on the bouncing ball.

"Hey, Dan," Jimmy yelled. "We need to

talk."

Suddenly Daniel rushed down the court and yelled at the referee. Jimmy had to run over and pull Daniel off the court.

"Dan, chill out!"

"He's a bad referee," Daniel snapped. His stomach grumbled. "Sorry. I get angry when I'm hungry."

"What do you like to eat?" Jimmy asked. "Sandwiches, chicken wraps, or maybe some juicy burgers?"

I watched Daniel's face very closely when Jimmy mentioned burgers. Daniel grinned, nodding his head. He didn't seem that interested in basketball anymore.

"I *love* burgers," Daniel said. "We always eat them at family barbecues." He licked his lips.

"Daniel, have you ever nicked any burgers?" Jimmy asked.

Daniel's eyes fell to the ground. His big grin turned upside down. Now he wouldn't look us in the eye.

"And have you ever stolen burgers from school?"

Daniel stuck out his tongue and looked like he'd be sick.

"Steal school burgers? No way! Those things are gross!"

"Why?" Jimmy asked. "They taste all right to me…"

"I tried the school burgers ONE time," Daniel said. "They were horrible! They had no seasoning, no tomato, no onions, no ketchup, no mustard, no lettuce, no salt and there definitely wasn't any pepper."

I hadn't thought about it before, but he was right. The dinner ladies never seemed to add any seasoning to food. They just dumped it into a giant pot and heated it up. That was it.

"So you haven't been stealing school burgers?" Jimmy asked.

"I'd rather eat that basketball than eat another disgusting school burger!" Daniel looked like he'd be sick again. "It took three takeaway burgers, two chocolate milkshakes, and a Yorkshire pudding to get the taste of ONE school burger out of my mouth."

"Do you have any idea who might've taken the school burgers?" Jimmy asked. "Ten of them—"

Daniel ran down the basketball court and started arguing with the referee. Jimmy and I rushed away before he came back. Daniel seemed like a nice boy, but he was a bit odd.

"I don't think he stole the burgers," Jimmy said. "The burger thief has to be Shelly or one of the other fat kids."

"You're right."

"Who should we talk to next?" he asked. "The girl with her friends, the bug girl or the mean-looking boy?"

I pointed at the fat white girl. She was sitting on the bench with her friends. They giggled over something on her mobile. They only took their eyes off the phone when a teacher came out. If a member of staff spotted the phone, it would be taken away and kept by the headteacher for a whole week.

When Jimmy and I reached the girls, they gave us a very mean look.

"Year Four brats," the fat girl spat. "Get lost."

Her friends laughed. Jimmy blushed and turned away. I didn't. I had a case to solve and not even mean Year Six students could stop me.

"We need to talk," I said to the fat girl. "If you don't help us, there will be serious trouble."

The Year Six girls laughed at us.

"Get lost, you cow!" the fat girl snapped. "You'll be in serious trouble if you don't get out of my face!"

"I don't have time to waste," I said. "Answer my questions and I'll leave you alone. But if you keep being mean to me then…"

"Then what?"

"Then I'll call my good friend Jamar, the Head Prefect. You know he's the smartest, most popular boy in Year Six."

The fat girl and her friends weren't laughing anymore.

"You wouldn't call Jamar on us, would you?" she asked.

"I would, but not just Jamar," I said. "I'll call our headteacher Mr Badal too. He won't be happy to hear you brought mobiles to school AND took them into the playground."

The girl looked shocked. Her friends ran off, leaving her alone. Good. I wanted everyone to know I wouldn't let mean people push me around.

"What do you guys want?" the fat girl asked.

"Let's start with your name," I said.

"Alicia."

Alicia patted the empty bench beside her, so Jimmy and I sat down. I took out my police badge so Alicia saw it. Her white cheeks turned bright pink and her eyes fell to the ground. When she spoke after that, her voice trembled.

"Alicia, ten school burgers went missing from the kitchen. Do you know anything about that?"

She shrugged, her eyes still on the ground.

"Don't make me call Jamar over here," I said. "He might bring Mr Badal with him."

"Okay, okay." Alicia threw her hands up. "I heard that Mr Badal ordered fewer burgers."

"Who told you that?"

"My friend Stacie was told by Sharon, who heard it from Jack. Jack said Pete told him about it. Pete heard it from his big sister, who's at that secondary school down the street. What's it called?"

"It doesn't matter," I said. "If she's at secondary school, how did she know that our school ordered fewer burgers?"

"That's a good question," Alicia said. "I hadn't thought of that...Maybe the other rumour was true, then."

"What other rumour?" I asked.

"If the other rumour is true then you won't ever catch the burger thief."

"Why not?" I asked, my heart pounding.

I had to solve the case! My boss would be very angry if I didn't. She was always mean to me. If I didn't solve the case, she'd be even meaner!

"The burger thief isn't just stealing burgers," Alicia said. "Loads of food has gone missing."

"How could one thief steal lots of food?" I asked.

"It's easy when you've got help," she said. "There isn't just one thief. There's loads of them, and you'll *never* catch them all…"

Chapter 3

I couldn't believe it. Alicia, the fat Year Six girl, said it wasn't just burgers going missing. She also said there were lots of thieves stealing from the kitchen.

"How many thieves are there?" I asked. "Two, three, five, ten?"

"Could be hundreds," Alicia said. "Maybe thousands someday."

I looked at Jimmy. He looked confused. So was I.

"Are you saying there's *hundreds* of thieves?" I asked. "That's impossible…"

If hundreds of people stole food from the kitchen, we'd *all* know about it. One person could sneak around without being spotted, but hundreds couldn't.

"How can hundreds of thieves hide in the kitchen?" I asked.

"It's easy when you're very, very small."

The only very small people at school were the nursery kids, but they didn't eat lunch with us. Maybe they'd stolen our burgers because our food was bigger and better than theirs?

"Nursery kids are stealing our burgers?"

"No, silly," Alicia cried. "I'm talking about the *mice* in the kitchen. You've seen the traps, right?"

Every student had. The mouse traps were always gone when teachers and parents were around. They didn't believe us when we told them about the traps. They thought we were making up stories.

"Mice are the burger thieves?" I said. "So it's not you?"

"To steal burgers, I'd have to go into that kitchen." Alicia's face turned paper white, her hands trembling. "I can't go in there…"

"Why not?" I asked.

"Last week, I saw one of the mice. It was watching me take a milkshake."

"What did it look like?" I asked.

"Like a normal chocolate milkshake, I guess."

"I was asking about the mouse, not the milkshake," I said. "Did you really see a mouse in the kitchen? Are you sure you weren't seeing things?"

"I'll *never* eat anything from that kitchen again," Alicia said. "I don't care if I have to eat boring sandwiches for a few months. Next year, I'll be at secondary school. I heard they have pizza, burgers, doughnuts, bagels and a fizzy drink fountain. I can't wait!"

Alicia skipped off with her friends. I didn't stop her. She wasn't the burger thief. How could she steal from the kitchen? She was too scared to go in there, and didn't eat school dinners anymore.

"Who else should we check?" Jimmy asked. "There's still the bug girl and that angry boy by the gates."

The fat, angry boy was still watching us. I wasn't looking at him, but I could feel his eyes on me. He didn't scare me, though.

"Let's talk to him," I said.

"You sure about this?" he asked. "That boy looks really mad about something…"

Jimmy sounded a bit scared, but a police officer has to be brave. We couldn't let the bad guys think we were afraid of them.

"Come on, Jimmy," I said. "Don't let him

scare you!"

"I'm *not* scared…"

When we walked over to the angry boy, he crossed his arms and shook his head.

"I know why you're here," he said. "I saw you talking to Daniel and Alicia."

"We need to talk about the missing burgers." I offered my hand to him. "My name is Mya Dove. What's yours?"

His white face turned dark red and he gritted his teeth hard. He turned away from me and muttered to himself. I couldn't hear what he was saying, but he sounded very angry saying it.

"We're police officers," Jimmy said. "If you don't tell the truth, we'll call Jamar, the Head Prefect. He'll tell Mr Badal—"

"Tell him what?" the boy spat. "I'm not talking and you can't make me."

He was right. We couldn't make him say

anything. He wasn't scared of Jamar or Mr Badal. He wasn't scared of us either.

The bell rang. We were out of time!

"I hope that you NEVER find those burgers," the boy cried. "And I hope more food goes missing soon."

He dashed across the playground and joined the Year Three line. His angry eyes glared at us as we walked to our class.

"Why's he so mean?" Jimmy asked. "I haven't done anything to him. Have you?"

"Nope," I said. "I've seen him around the lunch hall before. He's the only one who seems to love grapes as much as me."

"You have something in common with him," Jimmy said. "Maybe that'll help us? Scaring him didn't help at all…"

Sometimes scaring the bad guy works. It definitely worked on Alicia when I said I'd call Jamar.

But other times a police officer needs to be nice. If an officer is nice, the bad guy might be nice too.

"Jimmy, at lunch break I'll talk to him alone."

"You sure about this?" he asked. "He's really angry about something. I don't want him to hurt you."

I liked that Jimmy was worried about me. It showed what a great friend he was. But I felt that I had to do this part on my own.

"If anything bad happens, just wave me over," he said. "I won't let him make you cry or anything, okay?"

"He can't make me cry, but thanks anyway."

On our way back to class, I was nervous about speaking to the angry boy again. It felt like I'd done something to upset him, but I didn't know what…yet.

Chapter 4

At lunchtime, I spotted the angry fat boy who'd been mean earlier. He was glaring at the dinner ladies.

"I asked my friends about him," Jimmy said. "His name is Theo. He's in Year Three. He loves animals a lot. That's why he fell out with his friends. Now he eats by himself."

"They fell out over animals?"

"Yeah, after Theo told his friends that eating chicken is a bad thing."

"Why? What's wrong with chicken?" I said. "I'll ask Theo when I talk to him."

"Please don't talk to him by yourself," Jimmy said. "He looks so *angry*! Aren't you scared he might do something mean?"

"Nope," I said. "We're police officers and he's the bad guy. *He* should be scared of *us*!"

When the bell rang, I dashed outside to the playground and waited by the school gates. It was the spot where Theo had been earlier. I hoped he wouldn't be angry when he saw me there.

A few minutes later, he showed up. His eyes widened when he saw me, and then he looked really confused.

"What do you want?" he asked.

"Got any grapes?" I rubbed my belly. "I haven't had any in ages."

I'd seen him eating grapes before. Only a few of us ever seemed to bring them for lunch.

"Why don't you ask your boyfriend?" He

pointed at Jimmy, who was watching from the football pitch.

Jimmy was definitely *not* my boyfriend. I didn't have enough time for a boyfriend. I was too busy with my student and police jobs.

"Kissing girls is gross," Theo said. "Do you kiss your boyfriend? Yuck!"

My face felt so hot and my hands were warm. I couldn't let Theo know I was embarrassed.

"Do you have grapes or not?" I asked.

"I told you already," he spat, "ask your *boyfriend*! Eat his grapes, not mine!"

"My, um, boyfriend doesn't eat grapes. None of my friends do." I pulled a sad face. "I wish everyone ate grapes like you and me."

Jimmy and I were great friends. He wouldn't mind if I pretended to be his girlfriend. I only did it to solve the case…

"Your boyfriend doesn't eat grapes?"

"He doesn't like fruit and veg," I said.

"My friends don't eat fruit either." His eyes lowered to the ground. "They make fun of me for eating veg."

"Why?" I asked.

"I love fruit and veg, but other kids love chocolate and sweets. They laugh at me because I like different food."

Poor Theo. Some kids could be so mean. They picked on him for loving fruits. They probably picked on him for being fat, too. I hadn't been picked on, but I knew how it felt to be different.

Just like Theo, I was a kid who loved fruit instead of sweets and chocolate. Being different made me feel weird sometimes, like last year when we met Santa at the store. He offered me a doll, but I wanted a new police badge instead. The other kids laughed at me.

"Being different can be hard," I said, "but being different can be fun too!"

Theo's eyes lit up. He even smiled a little. His face wasn't red and angry like earlier. Now he looked paler and happier.

"Are you really a police officer?" he asked.

I showed him my badge.

"Wow..." Theo took a deep breath. "Sorry I was mean before. It was rude."

"We were a bit mean too," I said. "I won't call my Prefect friend or Mr Badal, okay? You aren't in trouble, but we still need to talk! Just you and me."

We sat together on a bench nearby. He reached into his trouser pocket and pulled out a packet of crisps. When he opened it, he stopped for a moment before offering me some.

"I don't know if you'll like them..."

I took one. It tasted amazing!

"I haven't seen these crisps at the shop," I said. "Where'd you buy them from?"

"From that new shop on the High Street. They only sell…um…Never mind!"

He looked away from me.

"You can tell me," I said. "I won't laugh at you, I promise!"

"The shop only sells…*vegan* food."

"Vegan? What's that mean?" I asked.

"Vegans don't eat animals," he replied. "No chicken, turkey, ham, bacon or beef."

"Whoa!" I couldn't imagine not having chicken anymore. "What DO you eat?"

"Vegetables, fruits, pasta, rice, bread, bagels, muffins, smoothies, nuts… As long as it isn't made from animals, I can eat it!"

Wait a minute, I thought. If Theo doesn't eat animals, he can't be the burger thief. He doesn't eat beef burgers because beef is made from cows.

"Theo, earlier you said you're happy about the stolen burgers. You even hoped more went missing!"

"Because I feel sorry for the cows," he said, his eyes welling with tears. "I saw some at the farm. I wanted them to be my friends, not my food."

I could see why he was sad. I'd be sad if someone ate our cat. Or my grandparents' dogs. Or our school's pet hamster.

"Theo, there's nothing wrong with being a vegan," I said, "but stealing animal food is wrong. It won't make people stop eating animals."

He nodded, his cheeks turning bright pink.

"If you show other kids your tasty vegan food, maybe they'll stop eating animals too."

"You're right," he said happily. "I'll eat with my friends like I used to. Then I can show them my tasty vegan burgers, vegan sausages, vegan cheese and lots more delicious vegan stuff."

Theo definitely didn't eat the ten missing burgers. He ate vegan food. But did he steal the burgers so other people wouldn't eat them? I asked him.

"I wouldn't do that," he said. "Like you said, nicking stuff is wrong."

That meant there was only one more fat kid to check. If it wasn't her that meant Shelly HAD to be the burger thief. There was no other fat kid to investigate.

Then I remembered something very important.

"Theo, earlier you said you wouldn't tell us something and that we couldn't make you."

His eyes slowly moved away from mine and stopped on the fat Asian girl. She was playing with bugs under the bushes, where Jimmy and I had seen her at breaktime.

"Did she say anything about the burgers?" I asked.

"Maybe…"

"Theo, *please* help me. I know you don't like us eating animals, but we both know stealing is wrong. If you didn't steal the burgers, tell me who did."

Theo edged closer to me, so I moved closer to him.

"She loves animals too, but she eats them," he whispered. "Well, the other day I saw her stuffing something into her pockets. It looked like plastic bags."

"The burgers could've been in there," I said. "I'll talk to her right now!"

After saying goodbye to Theo, I waved over Jimmy. He looked very surprised when Theo waved at him, but he waved back and smiled.

"Theo is a vegan," I said. "He doesn't eat animals."

"If he isn't the burger thief, we'd better check out the fat girl playing with bugs."

I told Jimmy she'd stuffed bags into her pockets. She could've hidden the stolen burgers in them.

"There's only one way to find out," he said. "Let's ask her!"

We crossed the playground and stopped by the fat Asian girl. She was busy playing with bugs and slugs, and barely looked back when I tapped her on the shoulder.

"Hey guys," she muttered, flipping away her silky braid. "Can't talk now. Busy looking for something!"

"What're you looking for?" I asked.

"Um, nothing…Just watching the ants carry food back to their home. Would you like to watch too? We can count the ants to see if any are…missing.”

Do ants go missing? I wondered. Do they get lost on the way home?

“No thanks,” I said. “We don’t have time to watch ants. We’re busy solving an important case.”

“Is that why you’re here?” she asked.

“Yes,” I said. “We’ve got some questions for you. It won’t take long. Then you can get back to your ant counting.”

The girl stood up, her chubby hands shaking. Her eyes filled with tears.

“What’s your name?” I asked.

“Shamima.”

“Shamima, is there anything you want to tell us?”

She nodded, then shook her head.

“Shamima, if you tell the truth now, I’ll try to get you less detention.” I patted her on the head. "Just tell the truth. You'll feel better when you do."

Shamima buried her face in her hands and cried. She might've been the burger thief, but I still felt sorry for her.

"Have you been stealing from school?" I asked.

She nodded.

"Tell us what happened, okay?" I said softly, patting her silky, black hair.

She took a deep breath and wiped her snotty nose on her arm. Tears trickled down her chubby cheeks while she spoke.

"When did you steal them?" I asked.

"Last week," she said. "Nobody else wanted them, so I took out a plastic bag and..."

"And what?" I asked.

"I stole them," she cried. "I stole them all..."

Chapter 5

I couldn't believe it! Was Shamima the burger thief? But my secret boss said it was Shelly, the fattest person at school. Shamima didn't look very, very fat. She looked like someone who could eat five burgers, not ten.

"You stole all ten?" I asked. "Really?"

"More than that," she said sadly. "Maybe fifty or a hundred. I lost count."

Shamima had stolen one hundred burgers from the school kitchen, but how? Wouldn't someone notice a hundred missing burgers?

She couldn't steal a hundred burgers by

herself, I thought. Maybe Shelly helped her?

"Did you steal them alone or did someone help you?"

"Alone," she said. "I took them all by myself. I know it was wrong but…I just didn't care."

She burst into tears. I wasn't supposed to feel sorry for bad guys, but I couldn't help it.

"Shamima, you've got to replace everything you stole," I said. "They were bought for the whole school, not just for you."

"I tried to replace them with the ones we've got at home, but ours are different. The ones at school are dark brown. The ones we have at home are dark red."

I'd never seen red burgers before. The only red on my burger was ketchup. Sometimes a slice or two of tomato as well.

"Just bring the red ones," Jimmy said.

"I'm sure somebody will eat them."

Shamima's eyes widened in horror. She started crying even harder now, her t-shirt soaked with tears. All her ant friends scattered away, probably scared by the noise.

"Did I say something wrong?" Jimmy asked, shrugging his shoulders. "Maybe it's a girl thing?"

"It's not," I said. "Shamima, what's wrong? Why're you crying? Jimmy didn't say anything mean!"

She was crying for no reason. People didn't do that unless they were *pretending* to cry.

Sometimes bad guys pretended to cry so we'd feel sorry for them. They hoped fake crying would get them a warning instead of detention.

If Shamima was fake crying, it wouldn't work on me. I was a very experienced police officer. I'd been solving cases for almost five years.

"Crying won't help you now," I said. "Taking what doesn't belong to you is wrong."

"I wanted to replace them," she sobbed, "but now I'm glad I didn't."

Shamima wasn't sorry about what she'd done. Now she was *happy* about it. She wouldn't be very happy when the Children's Police Force gave her weeks in detention.

"Shamima," Jimmy said softly, "you can still make things right. Just replace everything you stole!"

"No," she snapped. "Not after what you just said."

"I'm trying to *help* you," he said. "Replace everything you stole! Buy some new ones and cook them. Bring them to school tomorrow."

"You want me to...*cook* them?" she asked.

Her tears stopped. "You mean, put them in the oven or microwave?"

"Just don't burn them," he said. "No one likes burnt food."

Suddenly Shamima reached over and poked him in the nose. It happened so fast he couldn't move out of the way.

"You're both horrible," she cried. "How could I cook them? That's so mean!"

"We can't eat them raw," Jimmy said, rubbing the pink spot on his nose. "That'll make us sick."

"You shouldn't be eating them anyway," she spat. "That's gross!"

I stepped between them.

"Shamima, YOU stole them, so YOU need to replace them."

"I don't mind replacing them," she said, "but I will NEVER cook them!"

"I think she's a vegan like Theo," I said.

"I'm not," she said. "I do eat animals, but not gross ones like ants!"

"Ants?" Jimmy and I cried.

"You want me to cook ants and that's just gross!" she said. "I don't eat bugs and slugs. I just collect them."

Now I understood what was going on. Shamima wasn't talking about stealing burgers from the kitchen. She was talking about stealing ants from the playground!

"We thought you were stealing hundreds of burgers!" I cried.

"That would be silly," she said. "I put the ants in a jar. It had holes in the top so they could breathe. Then I put the jar in a plastic bag and…"

"And?" I said.

"When I got home, the ants were gone. They must've escaped on the bus!"

"You stole AND lost the school ants?"

"I know stealing is wrong but…could you let me off with a warning?" Shamima said. "Just this once!"

If we only gave her a warning, other kids might ask for warnings too. The Children's Police Force wouldn't be happy about that.

"It's not a big deal, right?" she said. "Nobody even noticed I'd taken them."

Stealing was wrong whether someone noticed or not. The ants belonged to the school, not her.

"You weren't even looking for an ant thief," she said. "That's because nobody noticed they were missing. Why? Because no one cares about the school ants. No one but me."

"Shamima, that doesn't make it right," I said. "You stole something from school. Stealing is wrong!"

Lunchtime would be over soon. We

couldn't waste time arguing over ants. We needed to find Shelly!

But first, I had to make a decision.

Should Shamima get detention for stealing ants, or should I give her a warning?

"Shamima, I'm sorry but—"

"It's okay," she said sadly. "I know what's gonna happen to me..."

Chapter 6

"How much detention will I get?" Shamima asked, her eyes filling with tears. "My parents will be so angry when they find out. I hope they don't take away my spider collection. Tara the Tarantula will miss me so much."

A tarantula? I thought. How could she keep a massive, ugly spider as a pet? Spiders always scared me. They loved to hide in dark, high places where it was hard to catch them.

"What's detention like?" Shamima asked. "Is it really scary?"

Only when Mr Badal showed up. I heard

he stood over the detention kids and glared at each of them He even brought a typed letter to their parents. Sometimes he posted it. Sometimes he didn't. It depended on how bad his mood was that day.

The detention kids were scary too. They were the naughtiest kids in the whole school. They got detention for really bad things like bullying, damaging school property on purpose, taking phones into exams, copying homework, saying rude words or disrupting lessons every day.

All Shamima did was lose some ants. Even if she'd lost a hundred of them, there were still hundreds, maybe thousands, left.

"I only stole the little ants," she said. "I didn't take the queen ant because she's the mum. The others can't live without her."

"What about the ants that escaped?" I asked. "Will they be okay?"

"They might come back…or they'll make friends with a new ant colony."

"Could the new colony join this old one?" Jimmy asked.

"Yep," she replied. "They'd become a super ant colony. Some supercolonies have MILLIONS of ants in them!"

She looked so happy, and then so sad.

"I won't see the new colony because I'll be in detention," she said. "I'm in big trouble, aren't I?"

Jimmy was watching me closely. He didn't say anything. I couldn't tell what he was thinking.

"Will you give me detention?" Shamima asked. "Please don't…"

It was time to make a decision: give Shamima detention or give her a warning. I had to make the decision myself because Jimmy wasn't helping!

"Shamima, you've been very naughty. Stealing ants is wrong." I gave her my mean face so she knew I was angry. "Lucky for you, we've got a burger thief to catch! But if I ever hear about you stealing school ants again, I'll handcuff you and take you straight to Mr Badal myself!"

"Thanks," she said. "I won't take any more ants without asking first."

"Don't thank me. I'm just doing my job."

"Good luck catching the burger thief," she said. "Why would someone steal burgers anyway? Couldn't they just buy some from the shop? They taste much better than the ones at school!"

Shamima wasn't the burger thief. She didn't like the taste of school burgers. Neither did Daniel. Alicia ate packed lunches because of mouse traps in the kitchen. Theo was a vegan, so he didn't eat beef burgers.

There was only one fat kid we hadn't questioned yet: Shelly Walters, our number one suspect. She was hiding somewhere at school so we couldn't find her.

Jimmy and I left Shamima with the ants. We stayed by ourselves so no one else would hear us.

"Why didn't you help me earlier?" I asked. "I didn't know what to do about Shamima."

"I think you did the right thing," he said. "Stealing is wrong, but nobody cares about the ants anyway. I'm sure she won't do it again, but if she does...I'll take her to detention myself."

He rubbed his pointy nose. It was pink and sore where Shamima had poked it.

"Shamima, Daniel, Alicia and Theo aren't the burger thief," I said. "Do we have any other suspects?"

"There's a really fat kid in Year Six, but he

was off sick when the burgers went missing."

"Anyone else?"

"A chubby girl in Year Two was on holiday when the burgers went missing," he said. "I don't remember any other fat kids…"

He was quiet for a moment.

"Mya, maybe we should check out people who *aren't* fat?"

"But only fat people eat a lot, right? That's why their bellies are really big." I puffed out my stomach and he laughed. "If the burger thief isn't a fat person, who could it be?"

"Maybe *nobody* is the burger thief," he said. "Maybe the dinner ladies didn't order enough burgers…"

That's what Shelly wanted us to think, but I wasn't falling for that!

"Jimmy, you said all the fat kids spoke to Nurse Mona, right?"

"Yes, before the burgers went missing."

"I need to see Nurse Mona and find out what's going on. Maybe she can tell me."

"If you need help, just let me know!" Jimmy said. "We're a team, remember?"

Jimmy dashed back to the football pitch. Everyone else groaned, still tired from the last match.

"Time to visit Nurse Mona," I said to myself. "I wonder what she knows about Shelly."

I hurried to Nurse Mona's room with lots of questions on my mind. Why did she have secret meetings with the fat kids? What did they talk about?

Outside Nurse Mona's room, I took a few deep breaths to calm down. My mind was buzzing! I had so many questions to ask and so little time to ask them.

I couldn't just walk in and ask questions. She would probably realise this was a police investigation. Then she'd tell other nurses and teachers about the case.

Soon students would start gossiping about the case too. Shelly would realise we were coming for her! Instead of going to detention, she'd run away from school, taking our burgers with her.

Worst of all, I'd never get my juicy green grapes! No case solved means no grapes. No case solved means no promotion. My boss might even take my badge away. Then what would I do?

"Calm down, Mya," I told myself. "Remember what Mum always says: Worrying doesn't solve anything. Just face your fears. It's never as bad as you think it will be."

You can do this! I thought. Let's go!

I knocked on Nurse Mona's door. There were papers rustling on the other side.

"Hello, nurse?" I said. "Can I come in?"

The door opened.

Instead of Nurse Mona, there was a different woman. Nurse Mona was fat, round and her face was all smooth. This woman looked very similar to Nurse Mona, but was skinny with a wrinkly face.

My heart started pounding faster. Who was this woman? Why was she here instead of Nurse Mona? Did Nurse Mona run away? Would she ever come back?

If Nurse Mona had left our school, we'd never know what Shelly told her in their secret fat meeting. The missing burgers would be gone forever. The case would stay unsolved.

My secret boss would be mad. The Children's Police Force would take my badge away. Worst of all, I'd never get my green grapes!

"Hi, sweetie," the nurse said. "Nice to see you again!"

Again? But we'd never met before. She looked familiar, but I didn't know her.

Well, I *thought* I didn't...

Chapter 7

"Hi," I said. "Where's Nurse Mona?"

The new nurse laughed. I didn't know what was so funny.

"I must speak to Nurse Mona," I said. "It's urgent!"

The nurse didn't laugh this time. She just stood there with a big smile on her face.

"Can you help me, please?" I asked.

"Oh, don't be silly!" The nurse pinched my cheek. "Who put you up to this?"

I couldn't tell her I was working for the Children's Police Force. It was top secret!

"Nobody," I fibbed. "Nobody put me up to this…"

"I bet it was that husband of mine," she said. "Well, you've made my day! Come in."

I looked past her but Nurse Mona wasn't there.

"When will Nurse Mona be back?"

"She's here!"

"Where?" Was she hiding in the cupboard? "I can't see her."

"Right here," she said, pointing at herself. "It's me!"

"Me who?"

"It's me," she cried. "Nurse Mona!"

I couldn't believe it! She was half the size she used to be! She definitely wasn't fat anymore. She had more wrinkles now, but looked younger than before. Maybe because she used to dress like my grandma. Now she dressed like my mum.

"Come in…Annie?"

"Mya."

"Mya, Mya, Mya…That's it! I remember your big brother William. He was always in here with cuts and scrapes and bruises." She chuckled. "Boys will be boys."

Will was different now. He didn't climb trees or play in the garden anymore. Now he stayed in his room for hours, playing online games and listening to loud classical music.

Nurse Mona opened the door wider and let me into her tiny room. Inside was an examination chair with a stool beside it. Behind the stool was a countertop with lots of medical stuff on it, like bandages and plasters.

Nurse Mona took out a blank piece of paper and found a blue pen. She sat on the stool while I sat on the examination chair.

"When was the last time I saw you?" she

asked. "I don't remember."

I did…

It was a year ago. After eating a tasty chocolate milkshake, I was sick all over the lunch table. It was gross and embarrassing!

Nurse Mona was so kind to me that day. I cried because people were pointing and laughing at me. She told me I had nothing to be ashamed of. Everyone got sick sometimes.

It was nice seeing her again, but a bit weird because she looked so…*different*. Her short, grey hair was now longer and dark brown. She also had on pretty make-up.

When she was very, very fat, she'd spoken quietly and kept her head down. Now that she was skinny, her voice boomed like the teachers' and she held her head high.

"What's the matter, poppet?" She took my hand and patted it gently. "I know I look different. I understand it takes some getting used to."

"Um, yes. It does."

"Sorry about that," she said. "Well, we'd better get on with things. Tell me what's the matter."

I couldn't ask her questions right away or she'd be suspicious. And I wasn't sure if I could trust her or not. What if she was working with Shelly? What if they were stealing burgers together?

I've got an idea, I thought. If I make her feel sorry for me, she'll answer all my questions.

"I don't feel so good," I said.

She checked my eyes with a torch, stuck a lollipop stick in my mouth, and looked in my ears for sticky wax.

There was a little bit in there...Yuck!

"Nurse Mona, I don't feel very well at all." I grabbed my stomach and squeezed tightly.

"I think it's the same thing Shelly Walters has. You remember her, right? You talked to her about...you know, that thing."

"What thing?" she asked. "And who's Shelly Walters?"

The bell rang.

"We'd better hurry, sweetie. Don't want you missing your lessons!"

"But I can't work like this!" I squeezed my stomach again. "It hurts!"

I put on my really sad face to make her feel sorry for me. Whenever I used my sad face at home, my parents let me break some rules. Last weekend, I got to stay up late and watch movies with William.

"Please help me, Nurse Mona!" I cried. "Just tell me what you told Shelly Walters. You remember her, right?"

"Did you say Shelly Walters? Shelly Walters...Shelly...Walters..." Her eyes lit up

and she smiled. "Oh yes! I remember her."
Then she frowned. "Poor little girl. So you
have trouble with food too?"

"Trouble with food?" I didn't know what
she was talking about, but she didn't know
that. "Yes! Could you tell me exactly what
you told Shelly? I think it could help me too!"

"I can't say too much, but I'll tell you what
I told her." She took my hand and patted it.
"Sweetie, there are lots of stereotypes about
fat people—"

"What is a stereotype?"

"A stereotype is a widely held belief about
a group of people. Stereotypes aren't always
true."

I took out my pen and paper to make
notes.

I asked, "So what fat stereotypes do people
think are true, but aren't?"

"Well, people assume all fat people are

greedy."

"Fat people are greedy," I wrote as she spoke. "Fat people like eating lots of food. What else, nurse?"

"People assume that fat people don't try dieting. They do. They just find it hard to control how much they eat."

"*You* lost weight," I said. "Why can't other fat people do it too?"

"They do try, trust me, but it's hard work, especially at my age." She sighed. "I had so many old, bad habits to change. It was hard, but I did it! I reached my goal!"

"How did you do it?"

"Gentle, fun exercise daily and lots of veggies with meals. No silly, dangerous diets and no exercising for hours a day. It took me two years to get fit and healthy because I wanted to go at my own pace."

I kept writing while she talked. She was

giving me great info on how fat people think. I could use the fat stereotypes to find proof that Shelly stole the burgers.

"Nurse Mona, stereotypes can be right, right? I mean they're not always wrong, right?"

"Stereotypes are based on real people, so yes sometimes they're true."

Nurse Mona looked very sad and her eyes fell to the floor. I felt sorry for her. It looked like she needed a big hug.

"People assumed I was lazy because I was fat," she said. "It's very hurtful when people assume the worst about you. They won't give you a chance because of your weight, skin colour, etc. It's a shame they're not sweet and kind like…"

"Like…?"

"Like *you*," she said. "You're such a friendly girl. Libby Smith told me all about you."

"She did? What did she say?"

"She told me how you became friends," Nurse Mona said. "Other kids thought she was mean, but you gave her a chance. She said you're a great friend!"

I blushed, my dark brown cheeks feeling really hot.

"Poor Shelly," Nurse Mona said. "I've seen her playing alone after school. I'm sure she would love to play with friends instead."

"She stays behind after school alone?"

"All alone."

Alone.

Alone after school...

That would be the perfect time to sneak into the kitchen and eat ten burgers. No one would see her do it. No wonder she'd gotten away with it for so long.

If anyone found her in the lunch hall, she

could just say she was waiting for her mum or something. She might get told off for being in the hall without permission, but no one would know about the ten burgers in her belly.

"What does Shelly do after school?" I asked.

"She plays basketball. All by herself, poor little darling."

I couldn't believe it. None of the fat kids played sports. In P.E., they just sat and watched everyone else. One of them always brought a note from their parents so the teacher would let them sit out games. When fat kids tried to play, no one played with them because fat people aren't good at sports, right?

"She's a great basketball player," Nurse Mona said. "I told her to join a team, but she doesn't handle the pressure in basketball games very well. Some people aren't comfortable in a competitive environment. They just want to have lots of fun."

"She plays basketball?" I looked her right in the eye. That makes it harder for the other person to lie. "So you've seen her play basketball?"

"…Yes."

She didn't look me in the eye when she spoke. That's how I knew she was fibbing.

"Nurse Mona, are you sure you saw her playing basketball?"

"Well…no," she said. "I mean she had a basketball in her hands. She was near the gym. I just assumed that she was playing."

"So you didn't actually see her play?"

"No, but she was taking a break at the time. She had a little snack to keep her energy up."

"What little snack did she have?"

"...I don't remember."

Nurse Mona swallowed a lump in her throat.

"Are you sure you don't remember?"

"Yes…I'm sure."

I tried to look in her eyes, but she kept looking away.

"Nurse Mona, you can tell the truth now or tell Mr Badal later. If you're honest now, I'll see what I can do to help you. Maybe you'll get less detention or something."

"No staff members *ever* get detention."

"Okay, then. If you tell the truth, I promise I won't write home to your parents."

"Darling, my parents are long gone..."

"Yeah, but they have to come back from holiday eventually. You can't hide a letter from school forever. My brother tried that but it didn't work."

"Darling, when I said my parents were

long gone I meant—"

"Just be honest," I said. "Tell the truth."

"I *am*," she said. "Shelly is trying very hard with her diet."

"You won't answer my question," I said. "Please tell me what snack she was eating."

"Losing weight is hard."

"What snack did she have?" I asked. "Grapes, apples, chocolate, what?"

"I still fall off my diet sometimes."

"Nurse Mona, what did you see Shelly eating? You can tell me or you can tell Mr Badal."

All the staff were scared of Mr Badal, our very mean headteacher. Sometimes he told the staff off just like he told students off.

"You really want to know what she was eating, don't you?"

I nodded.

Nurse Mona lowered her voice. It was so

quiet I could barely hear her.

"Mya…Shelly had a burger."

"I knew it!" I noted it down, so excited I could barely write. "You should've reported this. Why didn't you?"

"Because other people don't understand how tough losing weight is," she said. "Sometimes we need time off from dieting."

"Did you eat burgers when you dieted?"

"Sometimes I did," she said. "Burgers didn't stop me from losing weight, so they weren't a problem. Shelly having *one* burger isn't a problem either."

"So she had *one* burger, not ten?"

"Goodness no! She only had one."

Stealing one thing doesn't make it okay. It's still stealing.

"Nurse Mona, did Shelly eat a school burger?"

"Yes."

"How did she buy a school burger *after* school?" I asked.

"Let me explain," she said. "Shelly hadn't been eating much, so the dinner ladies were very concerned. They gave her a free school burger, just so she'd eat something. One free burger didn't hurt anyone, did it? Shelly just needed to eat something, anything!"

I could have reported Nurse Mona, but sometimes it's best to just let it go. People like her weren't the real bad guys. Besides, one day I might need her help again. She owed me for keeping her secret.

"I won't tell anyone about the free burger," I said. "If you ever help a bad guy or bad girl again, I'll go straight to Mr Badal."

"A bad girl?" She laughed. "What are you talking about? Shelly is *not* a bad girl."

"Shelly Walters is a suspect in a serious police investigation. Ten school burgers went missing last week. Did she mention that?"

Nurse Mona glared at me, her face turning dark red.

"So the fat girl took 'em? Sure. Always blame the fat kid. Shame on you!"

"I'm not blaming her because she's fat."

Yes, I was actually.

"I think Shelly is the burger thief because she's...she's..." I couldn't think of another reason. "Anyway, I shouldn't be talking about this with you. It's top secret!"

"Then this discussion is over," she snapped. "Here is the late note for your teacher. Goodbye."

I stormed out and headed back to class. When I gave Mrs Cherry the late note, she looked worried.

"I was wondering where you were," she said. "You went to see Nurse Mona? Are you all right, Mya?"

"I'm fine now, Miss."

I went and sat next to Jimmy. He showed me the page we were on, but I was too angry to read anything.

I was angry at Shelly for stealing food. I was angry at the dinner ladies for giving her a free burger. I was also angry at Nurse Mona for being mad at me. It wasn't *my* fault that fat people ate more food.

But then I looked over at Libby. She was reading with another girl. They looked like good friends.

Months ago, Libby always sat alone because everyone thought she was mean. But she wasn't. She was just really, really shy.

We were wrong about Libby, I thought. Maybe we're wrong about Shelly too? I've got to find out!

To prove Shelly was guilty or not, I had to know what she did after school. If she played basketball, I'd admit I was wrong and say sorry to her. But if she stole any burgers, I'd take her straight to Mr Badal.

It should've been easy to find out what Shelly did after school. All I had to do was stay after the last bell…but that was the problem. When the last bell rang, Daddy expected me outside. He didn't like me wandering around in school by myself.

But my dad wouldn't be a problem if Will picked me up instead. Will wouldn't mind if I stayed behind after school. He'd be too busy with his girlfriend to care.

I thought Dad would be fine with Will picking me up, but I was wrong.

Tomorrow morning, we'd have a big argument. Dad would make me so mad that I'd do something very mean to him. It would make him do something very mean right back…

Chapter 8

"Mya, we're gonna be late!" Dad yelled upstairs. "Will, get off the phone. You'll see your girlfriend at school."

"But Dad—"

"No buts, boy, get down here! And bring your sister!"

I waited patiently on my bed. We only had thirty minutes before school started, but I had to risk being late. I didn't want to ruin my perfect record – I'd never been late to school – but right now my police job had to come first.

Will pushed open my bedroom door and pulled a baseball cap over his fuzzy afro hair. He looked so scruffy and spotty, but he said teenage girls liked that.

I could smell his horrible aftershave from across the room. He said that teenage girls liked that funky smell too.

"Why're you sitting around?" he mumbled. "Get going!"

"I need your help," I said. "Can you do me a big favour, please?"

"No."

"Pretty please with sugar on top?"

"I like sugar, but I don't like you," he said. "I'm not helping you. Not after what you did to me."

"I've got to tell Mum and Dad when you're naughty," I said. "It's the rules! Good police officers always follow the rules. If I don't follow the rules, I'll lose my job!"

"Whatever, man! I'm outta here."

I laughed when he reached the door. He looked back, confused. I laughed again.

"What's so funny?" he asked. "Share the joke."

"I heard you on the phone last week…"

"And?"

"You were talking to your girlfriend…"

"So?"

"You said you're gonna get a tattoo."

He gulped.

"You're too young to get a tattoo! I'll tell Dad. You'll be in big trouble. He'll tell Mum. Then you'll be in even bigger trouble."

"William! Mya! Are you two coming down or not?" Dad yelled. "It's raining outside. The traffic will be crazy soon. Move it! Get down here! Now!"

"Coming Dad," Will said. He came over to me and sat down. "Okay, what do you want me to do? Make it quick! I've got a spot on my chin and it needs popping."

Gross. He said teenage spots were normal. I didn't mind normal spots, but teenage spots were MASSIVE. It was like he had a volcano on his face.

Every week, he'd pop the spots and let the goo spray on the bathroom mirror. He left it there. It made me feel sick every time I brushed my teeth!

"Will, tell Dad you'll pick me up after school or I'll tell him about your tattoo."

"Maybe I don't wanna pick you up!" He crossed his arms and turned away from me. "You cramp my style. Girls don't want some guy who hangs out with his little sister. I'm not a babysitter!"

"Fine, then. I'll just wait here for Dad and tell him all about your tattoo."

I got back into bed and pulled the covers

to my chin. It was so nice and cosy, and the sheets were fresh because Mum had washed them the day before.

"You're gonna be in big, big trouble when Mum and Dad find out."

"You're bluffing," he said. "You won't tell on me, right?"

I closed my eyes and pretended to snore.

"Okay, okay!" Will yanked me out of bed and tidied my white t-shirt and dark trousers. "What you up to now?"

"My police work is top secret. I can't tell just anybody." I tapped my nose. "One day you'll see my police cases on TV, but I can't tell you anything right now."

We went downstairs where Dad was storming up and down the hallway. He kept glancing at the clock on his phone. He hadn't even shaved. I hated when he did that. The fuzzy hairs hurt when I gave him kisses on the cheek.

He pointed at the clock on the wall and started moaning. He kept going on about being late and getting stuck in traffic. Any back chat would make him moan even longer, so we kept quiet and agreed with everything he said.

Eventually he stopped complaining. Now we only had twenty minutes before school. It seemed like enough time.

I nudged Will in the side. He nodded and stepped forward.

"What's going on?" Dad asked.

I thought Will would ask nicely if he could collect me after school. All I needed was Dad to say yes. He could stay home and work on his car. I could stay after the last school bell and catch the burger thief.

"Dad," Will said, "I'm picking her up later."

"Not happening," Dad snapped. "Last time you picked her up, you went to the police station."

"Not for being naughty," I cried. "We helped the police with a top secret case, remember?"

"That's what the lovely police officer claimed," Dad said. "Still not sure I believe her, though…"

"Dad, it won't happen again," Will said. "We'll come straight home, okay?"

"You are NOT picking her up, got it? Not until I trust you both again."

Oh no! If Dad picked me up, I couldn't stay behind after school. Then I wouldn't be able to prove Shelly was, or wasn't, the burger thief.

"Daddy, I need to stay behind after school," I said. "It's for a top secret case."

"Work on it at home."

"No, you don't understand!" I cried. "Someone is stealing from school."

"Then call the adult police," Dad said.

"But they're busy with bigger cases like catching people who steal cars. My case is a smaller one. Someone is stealing burgers."

"If it's a smaller case, you can solve it at breaktime and lunchtime. That's what you usually do."

"But—"

"You can't go sneaking around the school after the last bell!"

"But—"

"When the last bell goes, I expect to see you outside immediately, understood?"

"But...Yes, Daddy."

If he wouldn't let me stay after school, how could I catch Shelly? I had to stop her!

If Shelly got away with ten burgers, next time it might be twenty! Or thirty! Or a hundred! She might eat them all.

And she wouldn't stop there.

Once the burgers were all gone, she would start eating everything else in the kitchen. The yummy milkshakes, juicy fruits and roasted vegetables. Everyone else would be really hungry until they got home.

I couldn't let that happen. She had to be stopped!

"Daddy, I'm going to ask you one more time," I said. "Can I stay after school today?"

"Darling, I'm going to tell you one more time," he said. "No!"

Daddy was being so mean. He should've helped me solve the case. Instead, he was being stubborn. It made me so mad that I decided to do something *very* naughty…

I snatched the car keys from Dad's hand and ran into the kitchen. Before he got there, I hid the keys and sat at the table with my arms crossed. Now he'd know I meant serious business.

Dad ran in and opened his hand.

"Mya Dove, give me the car keys this instant."

"Nope." I shook my head. "I want Will to pick me up. It's really important for my case."

"Mya, don't make me tell you again. Give me the keys!"

"I am an officer of the law. This is for your own good."

It was true. When the burger thief was done stealing from schools, she'd steal burgers from houses. She might steal OUR burgers too! There'd be no burgers for Father's Day barbecues. Daddy wouldn't be happy about that.

"Give me the keys!"

I shook my head.

"Then I'll find them myself."

Dad checked the breadbin, the microwave, the washing machine, the oven, behind the telly, under the table, in my pockets, in my afro hair, in the cat's food bowl, in the plant pots on the windowsill, and almost every cupboard and drawer.

But he was *never* gonna find the keys. Why? Because I hid them somewhere he never goes: the cleaning cupboard.

"Mya, where are the keys?" Dad barked. "We have fifteen minutes to get to school. It's pouring down with rain, there's lots of traffic, I've got your mum's car to fix, I've got a splitting headache and…"

He grinned.

Uh oh…

You know that naughty grin parents give. It means they've thought of some way to punish you. You can't always outsmart them because they're older, so they know more than you. They were kids once, so they know what works and what doesn't.

Dad's smile widened.

I was *really* nervous now.

What did he have planned? It wouldn't be good. Would he take away my badge? Ban me from watching police shows for a month? Or, worst of all, would he tell Mum what I'd done today? If he did, I'd be in really, REALLY big trouble!

"You know what?" Dad said. "If you want Will to collect you after school, it's fine by me."

"Really?" Will and I both said.

"Of course! It means I can start work earlier than planned. See you later!"

Before Dad could leave the kitchen, I stood in the doorway with my arms spread. He tried to squeeze past but I wouldn't let him.

"Where are you going, Daddy?" I asked. "We need to go or we'll be late!"

"I'm not going anywhere," he said.

Dad sat down and turned on the telly. He put on a comedy show and burst out laughing. Then he poured himself some cereal and started eating.

"Um, Daddy," I said, "it's almost time for school. We'll be late!"

"That's not my problem," he said. "Your brother is taking you, not me."

"Why?" I cried.

"If Will can collect you from school, he can take you to school too."

"But he can't drive yet!"

"But he can walk. And so can you." Dad glanced at the clock on the wall. "Better hurry, Mya. Only thirteen minutes to go…"

Chapter 9

To punish me for hiding the car keys, Dad had refused to drive me to school. With only thirteen minutes before registration, it was impossible to walk there in time. If I was late, my perfect school record would be over. Dad knew that but didn't care.

"We won't make it in time!" I cried.

"You will if you run very, very fast. Get going."

"Nobody can go *that* fast!"

"What a shame," he said. "I could drive you if I had the car keys…"

I took the keys out of the cleaning cupboard and handed them over.

Dad laughed. "Never thought of that place."

He pulled me onto his lap and gave me a hug.

"Mya, I know this case means a lot to you, but you can't behave like that. Hiding the keys was wrong!"

"I'm sorry, Daddy!" I gave him a big hug. "It wasn't a very nice thing to do."

"All is forgiven," he said with a smile. "No more tantrums, all right?"

I nodded.

"So, Daddy, can I stay late after school today?"

"Not a chance," he said. "Whatever needs doing must be done at breaktime and lunchtime. Home time means time for home. No staying after school, is that clear?"

"But—"

"No buts, little lady." He ruffled my fluffy afro hair. "Come on. We've gotta go!"

A few minutes later, we were speeding off to school. Soon my class would be lining up outside. People would wonder where I was. They'd be surprised because I'd never been late before.

How would it feel to be late?

I'd be so embarrassed walking into class after registration. Angel and her friends would point and laugh. Jimmy and Libby would be sad because my "Never Been Late To School Ever" record would be over!

Worst of all, I'd get a very disappointed look from Mrs Cherry. It was the look she gave to all late students. They'd hang their heads in shame and people would point and whisper. At Parents' Evening, Mrs Cherry would show the attendance record and point out every time they were late. It was horrible!

I'm going to be late, I thought. Is this really happening? Me? Late?

Dad parked outside the school gates. I jumped out and ran off to class. Huffing and puffing away, I felt time ticking as I got closer and closer to being late.

I moved faster, our classroom door straight ahead. As I ran past the Year Five classroom, I spotted the clock on the wall.

Thirty seconds left!

Mrs Cherry stood up from her desk. She was heading for the classroom door. If anyone came after the door was closed, they'd be marked as late. Luckily I was close by, so I'd be just in time.

But then she started walking faster to the door. Was she trying to take away my "Never Been Late To School Ever" record? I was the only one in class who had it. Even Mrs

Cherry had been late a few times. Teachers aren't told off when they're late, so she always got away with it.

I wouldn't get away with being late, even though it was the first time.

Late was late. No excuses.

Don't close the door, I thought. Please give me more time! Please, please, please!

I was so busy panicking that I tripped over a coat on the floor. It must have fallen off the hook.

I fell flat on my face. It hurt. A lot. Soon tears were in my eyes.

"I'll help her, don't worry, Miss!" a familiar deep voice said.

Mr Murphy the caretaker stepped out of our classroom. He was dressed in dirty, baggy dungarees. He ran over to help me up.

"You all right?" he asked.

"I can't be late," I said, rubbing my sore

forehead. "I've got to go!"

Mrs Cherry appeared. She checked my face, her eyes stopping on my forehead.

"Mya, there's a bump on your head," she said. "You'd better see Nurse Mona."

"No, not her!" I stood up straight. "I'm fine, see?"

Mrs Cherry held my hand while I walked around a bit. My head hurt a little, but I felt okay.

"Mya, you know running isn't allowed inside the school building."

"I know, Miss. I just didn't want to be late."

"You're not late," she said. "Take your time and come in when you're ready. I still think you should see the nurse, though."

Mrs Cherry went back to class and took the register. I waited outside with Mr Murphy.

"Haven't I seen you before?" Mr Murphy asked, his black moustache twitching. "You look familiar…"

"Must've been someone else, Sir."

"Yeah, you kids all look alike," he said. "I see so many faces going from classroom to classroom. It's hard, no *impossible* to remember you all."

Mr Murphy was everywhere but no one got to know him. He'd come in, quickly fix stuff, and go. He wouldn't even stop for a quick chat.

But today was different.

"Thank you for helping me," I said. "I know you're very busy."

"I barely have time to sit down nowadays," he said. "It's nice to take a breather, you know?"

"Your job looks very hard, but it must be fun. You can go anywhere in school anytime you want."

"That's true," he said. "Sometimes I go into the playground when it's empty. It's so peaceful before you kids come out."

"I've never seen you out there."

"That's because I slip back inside," he said. "Moving around quietly is part of my job. It means I don't disturb others when they're working."

"So that's why we don't see you a lot," I said. "Because you move quickly and quietly like…like…like a ninja!"

"I guess so," he said. "Ninjas like me sneak around without being spotted. We're almost invisible!"

"That sounds so cool!"

"It is," he said with a grin. "Being an almost invisible, ninja caretaker means I hear and see crazy stuff you wouldn't believe…"

"Have you heard anything about our

school dinners?" I asked. "Some burgers went missing."

Mr Murphy looked away, his moustache twitching again.

Was he hiding something?

"I'd better be going," he said.

I couldn't let him leave. He knew something about the missing burgers.

Was Mr Murphy the burger thief?

He was an almost invisible, ninja caretaker who easily sneaked around. Maybe he crept into the kitchen, stole ten burgers and tiptoed away without being spotted.

To find out the truth, I needed to ask him some questions.

I flashed my police badge quickly.

"Sir, you can't go yet," I said. "We need to talk."

"About what, officer?"

"Have you heard anything about the

missing burgers?" I asked. "Yes or no, Sir?"

"You wanna know about the missing burgers, eh?" His dark eyes narrowed. "I knew you kids would figure it all out."

"Figure what out?"

Mr Murphy looked around to make sure we weren't being watched.

"Come closer," he said. "I shouldn't be telling you this but...I KNOW the burgers were stolen!"

The Children's Police Force was right! The dinner ladies *had* ordered enough burgers, but they were stolen!

"I'm glad you kids figured it out," he said. "The adults don't believe me when I tell them."

Poor Mr Murphy. I knew how he felt. I hated when people didn't believe my stories.

"I need your help," I said. "I want to catch the burger thief and give her detention!"

"Good on you," he said. "You're doing the right thing. They shouldn't get away with theft!"

"They?" I asked. "Is there more than one burger thief?"

"Yes. A whole family of thieves."

"Mr Murphy, do you know who stole the burgers?"

"Of course," he said, "but you won't believe me when I tell you…"

Chapter 10

"People think I'm wrong, but I know I'm not," Mr Murphy the caretaker said. "I know what really happened to those burgers…"

"Can you tell me, please?"

"The burgers were stolen by…huge, grey squirrels!"

"But squirrels don't eat burgers, do they?"

"I know it sounds crazy, kid, but it's true! Squirrels don't just steal nuts. I've seen them steal bird food, doughnuts, chocolate bars and Christmas lights. If it's not nailed down, they'll snatch it!"

I found it hard to believe a squirrel wanted burgers. They ate seeds and nuts, not juicy beef burgers.

"How could a squirrel get into the kitchen?" I asked.

"There's air vents and all sorts of tiny tunnels behind the walls. I've been trying to patch up any holes, but the little critters bite their way through!"

I tried to imagine a squirrel eating a burger, but it just seemed so silly! How could they eat a burger without any ketchup, fried onions or a bun?

"Mr Murphy, do you have any other suspects?"

"Well, if squirrels didn't steal the burgers then it must be someone else." His scruffy, black moustache twitched. "I think I know who it is."

"Go on…"

"A chubby, blonde kid." He checked over his shoulder. "Anyway, I've said too much already. Time for me to go."

"Do you have to?" I cried.

"I've got a toilet to unblock. I really wish people would save the big poos for home, ya know?"

Yuck!

Don't tell anyone but I made one of those big poos before. I couldn't help it! I'd eaten too many grapes and they popped out the other end. I reached the loo seconds before the poop explosion.

Afterwards, I locked myself in the toilet stall and wouldn't come out until everyone else had gone. Luckily the other girls never knew it was me. At least, I hope not...

"Wait a sec, Mr Murphy. Are you talking about Shelly Walters, the fat basketball player?"

"Yeah, sure. The so-called basketball player." He sniggered. "If she plays basketball for exercise, it ain't making a difference. I guess she's still eating too many of those *horrible* school burgers."

"Did you see her steal any burgers?"

"No, but she could've done it when I wasn't around," he said. "I can't keep an eye on every kid at the same time. There's too many of you."

"Do you have any other suspects besides Shelly and...the squirrels?"

"If it wasn't squirrels or the really fat girl, then the school's just getting healthier. Government initiatives and all that."

"Government initiatives? What does that mean?"

"It means the government wants to achieve a certain goal, for example, get more people to eat vegetables."

He lowered his voice before speaking again.

"The prime minister wants more veg in schools. More fruit too. The government wants every headteacher to cut down on school burgers, bit by bit. Soon there'll be nothing left but plain carrots and wholemeal bread."

Plain carrots without any seasoning? No way! I didn't mind plain broccoli, but not plain carrots. That was taking things too far!

"Mr Murphy, maybe Shelly heard about the government initiative too? Maybe she was really angry about eating more veg and fewer burgers?"

"Or it made her really sad," he said. "My missus always eats when she's sad. It makes her feel better...for a while, but not for long."

"Why?" I asked.

"Because eating to feel better is a bad

idea," he said. "The only problem food solves is hunger. It doesn't take away sadness, pain or anything else."

Mrs Cherry came out of class, looking very confused.

"Have you been out here this whole time?" she asked. "I thought you'd gone to the nurse?"

"I feel okay, Miss."

"I'll keep an eye on you, just in case," she said. "Come inside, dear."

"Get going, kid," Mr Murphy said. "And good luck with that thing we talked about. I hope you catch her!"

I said goodbye and went to my desk.

We had science on Tuesday morning, but I couldn't think straight. My mind was stuck on Shelly Walters and what Mr Murphy had told me.

Was Shelly eating ten burgers because she

was sad? Did she eat to feel better? Maybe the government initiative upset her because soon all school burgers would be gone?

I'd be sad too if a government initiative took away all my grapes. I'd eat loads before they ran out. When they were gone, I'd miss them so much!

Wait a minute...Was I feeling sorry for the bad guy?

Shelly might've been stealing from school, but it wasn't that simple. Maybe she wasn't stealing to be mean. Maybe she was stealing because she was sad. She could've been eating burgers to feel better.

But stealing was wrong. Wrong is wrong, whatever the reason is. Shelly was still a bad guy. I was still a police officer. It was my job to follow the law and make sure everyone else did too. Even if she felt sad, she shouldn't be stealing. It wasn't fair on everybody else.

I've got to catch her, I thought, but when? Dad said I can't stay after school!

If I couldn't catch her after school, I'd have to try at breaktime. It was the only free time I had to solve the case.

When I did catch Shelly, I'd take her straight to detention, even if it made her cry.

I thought I had it all figured out. At the time, I didn't realise Jimmy had been investigating Shelly himself. He'd found out something shocking and couldn't wait to share it...

Chapter 11

Usually P.E. was an easy class, but that Tuesday morning it was *really* hard. I just couldn't focus! All I could think about was Shelly and the missing burgers.

"Mya, are you all right?" Mrs Cherry asked. "You don't seem like yourself today..."

She was right. Today I couldn't hit any balls when I played tennis. Usually I hit them so hard they flew past everyone.

"Maybe you should sit down for a bit," Mrs Cherry said, pointing at a bench. "You took a bad fall earlier, remember?"

Feeling down, I sat on the bench and watched everyone else have fun.

"Mya," Jimmy said. "How's it going?"

He sat beside me.

"Jimmy, I think Shelly is stealing burgers, but I don't have any proof."

"Without proof, we can't send her to detention," he said. "She'll get away with stealing!"

"*If* she is the burger thief," I said. "It could be someone else…"

The burger case that looked so simple was getting harder. Was the burger thief Shelly or a very naughty squirrel? I had no idea what to think anymore!

"Did you find out anything?" I asked. "I know you're busy and everything but…I need help."

"I'm never too busy for you," he said,

smiling. "You know Shelly stays behind after school, right? I asked a friend to look around after the last bell. He passed by the lunch hall and guess what he saw?"

I leaned in, my hands sweaty with excitement. We finally had a witness! Maybe the witness saw Shelly stealing burgers? That would be the proof we needed!

"What did the witness see?" I asked.

"My friend, the witness, saw Shelly talking to the dinner ladies. They gave her a box of frozen burgers."

"What happened next?"

"Don't know," he said. "My friend couldn't hang around because Mr Badal spotted him. My friend almost got caught, you know?"

Mr Badal was the headteacher, so no one wanted to make him mad. He didn't like students staying after school.

"I can't believe they gave Shelly a box of frozen burgers," I said. "Does she cook them in the school kitchen? Is that allowed?"

"She probably takes them home. Maybe she's having a barbecue or something? We always buy lots of burgers and sausages before a barbecue."

I couldn't believe it. So Shelly WAS bad! And just when I'd given her a chance. She didn't deserve it. She wasn't just stealing ten burgers from the kitchen. Now she was taking whole boxes of them!

She was smart for getting the dinner ladies to help. When someone noticed the missing burgers, the dinner ladies could blame Mr Badal. He could blame the prime minister's "government initiative" for taking away our burgers. But no one would blame Shelly, even though she was the one behind it all!

"Will your friend be a witness in

Detention Court?"

"Court? Where lawyers and judges are? No chance. He's got exams to study for. He hasn't got time for court. You know how busy Year Six is."

I'd heard. Their exams were very, very important. If they got great results, they'd move to a bigger, better school. If not, they'd stay at our school forever and ever...or so I heard. Not sure if it's true, though.

If Jimmy's Year Six spy was too busy to help, I needed witnesses who had lots of free time. If they helped me, the case would be solved quickly. I'd be eating juicy, green grapes by early Thursday morning. Yum yum!

But I wouldn't get my grapes if I didn't prove Shelly was the burger thief. I couldn't prove she was guilty if I didn't have witnesses to help.

And not just any witness. People believed witnesses who were kind to others. People found it hard to believe naughty, mean witnesses because they might be telling fibs.

"Who can be our witness?" I asked.

"Someone, or some kids, who always tell the truth. Kids who always follow the rules. Kids who always stay out of trouble. Kids like…us."

"You and me?"

"We'd make great witnesses!" Jimmy cried. "People think police officers always tell the truth. They'll trust us."

I'd never been a witness before. I was looking forward to it. Soon I'd be in Detention Court and tell everyone what I'd seen.

"You're right," I said. "We'll be witnesses. We'll catch Shelly stealing and tell the Detention Court what we saw. We're police officers. Everyone believes us."

Jimmy nodded in agreement. "We'll get her at lunchtime...I hope."

He hoped? I hadn't expected that. Jimmy always believed we'd solve the case and catch the bad guys. We couldn't give up when hundreds of kids were counting on us.

So why was he unsure today?

"Jimmy, talk to me. What's up?"

"Look, Mya, I'm just..."

"I know. I've been wrong before but this time is different. I can feel it."

"Just wondering, that's all. I mean, Shelly seems all right to me. Haven't heard anything about her being mean. She just stays by herself, all alone..."

Jimmy looked really sorry for Shelly. It made me feel guilty.

Maybe she wasn't a burger thief. Maybe the school really had just ordered fewer burgers and more veggies. Maybe Shelly was getting the blame for something she didn't do. Nurse Mona saw Shelly with one burger, but that didn't mean she stole the other nine, right?

"You don't think she's the burger thief, do you?" I asked.

Jimmy shook his head.

"What about the witness? He said the dinner ladies gave Shelly a box of burgers."

"GAVE her," he said. "If someone gives you something, it's not stealing. Maybe the dinner ladies stole the burgers but didn't tell Shelly they were stolen."

Maybe he was right.

Maybe he was wrong.

Either way, I couldn't go to my boss and tell her that Shelly wasn't guilty because Jimmy said so. I needed proof.

"Okay, Jimmy. If Shelly isn't guilty then

we've got to prove it."

"Let's spy on her at lunchtime," he said. "If she doesn't steal any burgers, we'll know she isn't the burger thief."

"But if she *does* steal some burgers…"

"Then we'll be witnesses," he said. "After we go to Detention Court, Shelly will be in serious trouble. She'll definitely get detention."

I didn't want Shelly to be in detention if she was innocent. It wasn't right to punish people who weren't guilty. If someone else stole the burgers, *they* should go to detention, not Shelly.

Poor Shelly, I thought. All those bullies blaming her just because she's fat. How mean! Well, I wouldn't let it happen anymore.

At lunchtime, I'd catch the real bad guy stealing burgers. Then I'd make the whole school say sorry to Shelly, just like they did to Libby. No one would pick on any more quiet or fat people. I wouldn't allow it!

"Come on, Jimmy!" I said. "We're gonna prove Shelly is innocent."

Jimmy smiled when I said that. It made me happy seeing him happy.

"Thanks for giving Shelly a proper chance," he said. "I don't like seeing people get picked on, you know?"

Jimmy was one of the best police officers at school. If he thought Shelly wasn't the burger thief then he was probably right. That's what I thought anyway.

Little did we know that we were about to catch Shelly stealing, but she wouldn't be taking any burgers...

Chapter 12

At lunchtime, Jimmy and I rushed out of class. On the way to the lunch hall, we looked out for anyone suspicious. No one was acting strangely, but that didn't mean the burger thief wasn't around.

In the lunch hall, Jimmy and I sat at the back to keep an eye on everyone. People were eating, drinking and chatting. Only the dinner ladies were going in and out of the kitchen.

"Nothing suspicious yet," Jimmy whispered. "I don't see any burgers being nicked."

"Where's Shelly?" I asked. "Can you see her anywhere?"

Jimmy pointed straight ahead. I followed his finger to a lunch table near the kitchen. A dinner lady stopped by the table, patted a blonde girl on the head, and hurried off.

"That's Shelly," Jimmy said.

Shelly was a blonde, white girl like Angel, but three times bigger. She was staring at a glass of water in front of her. Every so often she'd take a sip, a tiny one, and then stare at the water again.

"Isn't she hungry?" Jimmy asked. "I know *I* am!"

"She must be starving," I said. Shelly rubbed her big belly, making it jiggle. "See. She's hungry. Why doesn't she just eat something?"

I was hungry too, but I didn't have time

to eat. I had to keep one eye on the kitchen and another on Shelly. It's hard to make each eye look in different directions.

"I don't think she's the burger thief," Jimmy said. "She isn't eating burgers or anything else."

"Then it has to be someone else...Keep looking!"

While I looked around, I got a bit bored. To pass the time, I started imagining the real burger thief. I pictured him as an angry-looking boy whose stomach growled when it was empty.

Then I imagined the burger thief sneaking into the kitchen with a massive backpack. He'd creep into the freezer and grab enough burgers to fill a shopping bag or two. He might even throw some burgers on the grill and eat them right there.

When the burger thief was busy cooking,

Jimmy and I would rush over and flash our police badges. To escape, the burger thief would run to the back door. That wouldn't work, though. Jimmy was the fastest kid in school. He'd reach the door first and stand in front of it, blocking the way out.

After we handcuffed the burger thief, we'd search his pockets for proof. Inside we'd find buns, ketchup and fresh onions. Everything he needed for the perfect burger!

"I won't be in detention forever," the burger thief would cry. "When I get out, I'll be back! Next time I'm taking the chocolate milkshakes too!"

"Then we'll catch you again," I'd say. "You can count on that!"

After handcuffing the real burger thief, we'd tell everyone that Shelly wasn't guilty. They would ALL have to apologise. I would too. I'd been mean to her just like everyone else, and all because she was fat.

I guess Nurse Mona was right, I thought. Stereotypes aren't always true.

"Mya, you okay?" Jimmy asked, nudging my arm with his elbow. "You've been quiet for a bit."

"Sorry, I was daydreaming about the real burger thief," I said. "I can't wait to see the look on everyone's face when they find out Shelly isn't guilty."

"Well, if we're going to catch the real burger thief, he'd better show up soon because…" The bell rang. "Too late. We're out of time."

Lunch was over.

Everyone was dumping leftovers, scraping their trays, sucking out the last juice from cartons, and closing lunchboxes. Soon they were lining up to go outside and play.

Shelly stayed in her seat, still sipping her

water. She had loads left even though she'd been drinking for half an hour.

Suddenly Shelly looked up and we locked eyes. Her eyes were puffy and pink like she'd been crying. Why hadn't someone got her a tissue or given her a hug?

Then her eyes slowly moved to the kitchen. She was looking around but no one was there. A moment later, she looked back at me. Her eyes kept going from the kitchen to me and back.

"What's she doing?" I asked.

"She's waiting for us to go," Jimmy said.

"Can she hear us from over there?"

"Dunno, but she can definitely see us."

I held an apple in front of my mouth so she couldn't read my lips. Some people are very good at lip-reading. It means they know what you're saying even though they can't hear you.

Jimmy copied me, but he held a banana in front of his mouth. We looked a bit silly, but at least she couldn't read our lips anymore.

"Is she still looking?" I asked, trying not to look.

Jimmy pretended to sneeze, and quickly looked over at Shelly. She turned away, finally letting go of her water.

"Get down," Jimmy whispered. "Now's our chance!"

We dropped to the floor, pulling our lunchboxes down with us. Slowly we peered between the chair legs and spotted Shelly getting up.

"If she's not the burger thief," I whispered, "she'll go outside and play."

Jimmy nodded, looking nervous.

"Do you still think someone else is the real burger thief?" I asked.

"…Yes."

Jimmy wanted to give Shelly a fair chance. I did too.

To prove Shelly wasn't guilty, all she had to do was leave the lunch hall. If she didn't sneak into the kitchen and steal burgers, it would prove someone else was the burger thief.

Shelly stood up and turned to the door. I expected her to walk outside.

"She'll be going out soon," Jimmy whispered. "See? She's NOT the burger thief! Everyone was wrong about her."

But Shelly didn't go outside.

Instead, she crept into the kitchen. Jimmy and I watched in horror, still hoping she'd turn back. She peeked over the serving counter, her hazel eyes on the door.

Jimmy and I stayed under the table. We kept perfectly still, watching Shelly in silence.

A moment later, she pulled out a food tray

covered in clingfilm. She tore off the clingfilm and grabbed a handful of salad. She held it to her nose before gobbling it down.

A whole lettuce leaf went straight down her throat. Several tomato slices followed. And cucumber, rocket leaves, spinach, onions, carrots, celery, red and green peppers, mushrooms, watercress…

"Whoa," Jimmy whispered. "Is she gonna stop for air?"

She did. Eventually. Not before finishing the WHOLE tray of salad.

When Shelly was done, she ran out the lunch hall in tears. Even though she was very naughty for eating all the salad, I still felt sorry for her. Why? She was just another bad guy, right?

"Well, Mya, you were right. Shelly is stealing food."

I wasn't happy about being right. A part

of me wished I'd been wrong…

"Well done, Mya."

"For what?"

"You solved another case," he said. "Good job!"

Solving a case usually felt AMAZING, but this time I felt sad…

"Do you want to handcuff Shelly or should I do it?" he asked. "I don't mind either way."

"I can do it," I said. "I'll arrest her."

"Okay, cool. Let me know—"

"Maybe you should do it?"

"That's fine," he said. "I'll just—"

"Actually no, it's my case. I'll do it."

"Great, just tell me—"

"You can do it if you want to," I said. "Do you want to?"

"I don't mind—"

"Or do you want me to do it?" I asked.

Now Jimmy looked *really* confused. It was my fault. I just couldn't make up my mind! Should I handcuff Shelly or not?

I wasn't scared of handcuffing someone. I'd done it lots of times.

But this time was different.

It was the first time the bad guy was upset. I couldn't go out and arrest her when she was crying like that. I'd feel bad. I'd *look* bad too. I couldn't have everyone feeling sorry for the bad guy because I made her cry.

"So, Mya, are you going to arrest her or not?"

I didn't want Jimmy to know I felt sorry for a bad guy. Police officers aren't supposed to feel sorry for people who break the rules.

"I won't arrest her," I said. "Neither will you."

"Why not?"

"My secret boss said Shelly stole *burgers*,

not salad. Besides, no one will believe a fat person is stealing salad. Burgers and fries and chocolate and sweets, yes, but not veggies. Fat people don't eat salad, right?"

"My mum eats salad to get fit before our holidays. She gets fatter when she stops eating salad."

"See! Shelly would be skinny if she just ate salad." I leaned in, just in case we were being watched. "She knew we were hiding under the table. That's why she ate the salad instead of the burgers."

"Shelly is smarter than we thought," he said. "Maybe she knows that we're investigating her?"

Sometimes a bad guy knows the police are watching. It doesn't matter how hard you try to hide, they might still find out they're being investigated. It doesn't stop us from catching them, though. Once we have enough proof, the bad guys are sent to detention!

And that's where Shelly was going.

If she was very lucky, the Children's Police Force might feel sorry for her. If they did, she wouldn't be in detention for more than a week. But she wouldn't get detention if we didn't prove she was stealing burgers.

"Jimmy, we tried hiding from her but it didn't work! She knows we're watching her."

"What should we try instead?"

"No more sneaking around," I said. "Tomorrow, we'll talk to her."

We wouldn't just talk to Shelly. We'd also set a trap to catch her! Then everyone would know she ate a lot more than salad.

"Jimmy, tomorrow we'll need a burger. The biggest, tastiest one you can find. Make sure you don't eat it yourself."

He gulped. "I'll try not to..."

"We'll talk to Shelly. I'll need you for the

inter….interro…"

"Interrogation."

"Exactly," I said. "We'll ask her lots and lots of questions. She'll be very confused! To confuse her even more, we'll act like two completely different officers."

"How?"

"One of us will be a nice, friendly police officer. The other one will be an angry, mean police officer. Which one would you like to be?"

"Good cop, bad cop, you mean?" He stopped to think. "Um...I want to be the good cop!"

"No fair," I cried. "*I* wanted to be the good cop!"

"Then you should've picked first!"

He grinned. I rolled my eyes.

"Anyway, Mya, when should the interrogation start?"

"At morning breaktime," I said. "We'll find Shelly in the playground and get her to admit she's been burger stealing."

By working together, Jimmy and I would finally solve the case. All we had to do was stick to my simple plan.

To catch Shelly, first we'd ask her lots and lots of hard questions. Next, we'd use some burgers to prove she was the burger thief. Finally, we'd take all the burger stealing proof to the Children's Police Force. They'd give Shelly detention, and give Jimmy and me a big reward.

"Get ready for tomorrow," I said. "Shelly is a really smart bad guy. We've got to be smarter to beat her!"

When we went outside, Jimmy ran off to practise his good cop stuff. I sat on a bench and thought of mean things a bad cop would say.

"This interrogation will be easy," I told myself. "Shelly can't beat a great team like Jimmy and me."

It was very helpful having Jimmy on my side. The problem was, Shelly had time on hers...

Chapter 13

After a fun lesson about West African music, our class went out for morning breaktime. I was so excited about solving the case that I skipped all the way to the playground. People looked at me funny, but I didn't care.

Today Jimmy and I would prove Shelly ate burgers, not just salad. To prove it, we needed some burgers, so I brought one from home. My brother cooked it for me, but he didn't do it for free. I had to pay him two whole pounds.

In the playground, Jimmy spotted Shelly

sitting under the climbing frame. Her head was in her hands. It looked like she was crying.

She's pretending, I thought. I'm not falling for it!

"You ready?" Jimmy asked me.

I nodded.

"Good," he said. "You're the bad cop, remember?"

How could I forget?

In case you don't know, good cop bad cop is an old trick police officers play on bad guys.

The good cop acts nice so the bad guy thinks they're friends. People always tell secrets to friends. They don't tell secrets to the bad cop, though. Bad cops are really mean to make good cops look really kind.

Basically, Jimmy would act like a nice police officer. I would act like a mean one.

"Let's do this," he said. "You ready?"

"Whatever," I snapped. "Get over there before I get *really* angry!"

"Whoa, that was mean. You're good at this bad cop thing!"

I didn't thank him. Mean cops don't say thanks when they get a compliment. Instead I gave him an angry face before storming over to Shelly.

Shelly jumped from fright when she saw us. I marched over and gave her the meanest look I could. It was the same look Mum gave when I didn't do my homework.

Jimmy smiled and offered his hand to her. She shook it, not smiling back. When she tried to shake my hand, I wagged my finger. She looked sad about that, but that was a good thing. She was supposed to like Jimmy (good cop), not me (bad cop).

"James, sit down," I snapped, "or I'm gonna get really, really angry."

"Sorry, Mya!" he cried.

"Call me Detective Inspector Dove!" I gritted my teeth so hard it hurt. "Don't make me tell you again."

"Sorry, Detective Inspector Dove!" He sat down beside Shelly. "Can you call me Officer—"

"No," I snapped. "Now be quiet."

I banged my fist on the climbing frame and pointed at Shelly. She moved away from me, her hands shaking.

"Miss Walters," I said, "where were you at 8pm last night?"

"In bed. Sleeping."

"Any witnesses?"

"Well, yeah, my mum. She read me a bedtime story."

"About what?"

"A dragon."

"What kind of dragon?" I spat.

"What do you mean?" she asked. "Just a normal dragon."

"What KIND of normal dragon?" I snapped. "A big or small one? Was it mean or nice? What colour was it? Maybe it was bright green like a *salad*? Or maybe it was dark brown like a *burger*?"

Shelly was starting to sweat. Good. That meant she was nervous. Nervous bad guys are more likely to admit to being naughty.

Jimmy took Shelly's hand and squeezed it gently. She blushed.

"You said you were asleep at 8pm last night," Jimmy said. "Did you read a bedtime story before bed?"

She nodded.

"Cool! What's your favourite bedtime story?"

"It's a bit scary for bedtime but...I'd say Booger King by Zuni Blue! I think it's based on a true story..."

"Oh, I've read that one," Jimmy said. "The boy's picking his nose and a massive booger comes out to attack—"

"Miss Walters!" I cried. "You haven't answered my questions!"

"What did you ask? I've forgotten…"

I'd forgotten too…

"Let's talk about something else," I said. "Tell us where the missing boogers, I mean the missing *burgers* are."

"First you asked about dragons, then boogers, and now burgers?"

"Are you being cheeky?" I snapped.

"No…"

Shelly looked away. Her face was bright pink and sweaty, just like Jimmy's when he played football.

"Shelly, please talk to us," Jimmy said. "If you tell the truth, you might get less detention. Just tell me what really happened. Did the ten burgers fall into your bag by accident?"

Shelly snatched her hand away from his. He put on a sad face that made me feel sorry for him, even though I knew he was faking it.

"Sorry," Shelly said, taking his hand back. "I'm just...I'm fed up with everyone blaming me when food goes missing."

"If you didn't take the school burgers, who did?" I asked.

"Mice in the kitchen," she said.

"Or maybe it was *you* in the kitchen," I said. "You ate the burgers all by yourself."

Shelly's mouth was open, catching flies my gran would say.

"I don't eat burgers anymore," Shelly said. "I'm on a diet. A no food diet. I'm not eating anything!"

That didn't sound very healthy. We all get

hungry after a while. It's perfectly normal.

"Miss Walters," I hissed, "you said you don't eat, but you were seen eating salad yesterday. Don't ask who saw you! We won't tell!"

She rolled her eyes.

"You don't have to tell me. I saw you both hiding under the table, playing with your lunch."

I knew it! She HAD seen us! What a smart girl. Well, too bad I was smarter.

"Miss Walters, did the dinner ladies give you a box of frozen burgers?"

Her mouth gaped open.

"How'd you know about that? Nobody else was there!"

Jimmy's friend in Year Six had been there. Luckily Shelly and the dinner ladies hadn't seen him.

"So it DID happen!" I cried. "You stole

the school's frozen burgers."

"They made me take it," she said. "They were worried about me not eating. They thought my family didn't have enough money for food, so they gave me some. It was leftovers nobody wanted. The burgers would be in the bin if I hadn't taken them."

I didn't believe her. Even if the dinner ladies *did* give her free food, that wasn't allowed. She had to pay for it like everyone else.

"Miss Walters, why is the staff being so nice to you?" I asked. "You get free food from dinner ladies, secret meetings with Nurse Mona..."

"That's none of your business," she snapped.

"You're right, it's not," Jimmy said. "Anyway, I'm sure your top secret talk with Nurse Mona went well. I hope it did."

"It went great," Shelly said, smiling at him. "I felt so much better after talking to her."

"I'd love to hear all about it but…Nah! It's not my business, right?" Jimmy patted her chubby hand. "Forget I said anything, okay? I was just being nosy!"

"I don't mind telling *you* anything."

She took Jimmy's hand and squeezed it. His face turned bright pink and she giggled.

I didn't find it funny…

"James," Shelly said, "Nurse Mona gave me great tips on getting fit. I told her I don't eat food. She wasn't very happy about that. She said not eating is dangerous."

"She's right," Jimmy said. "My dad says food is like petrol in a car. It keeps us going."

"You really don't eat? That's a big fat lie!" I spat, still in bad cop mode. "How can you be fat if you don't eat?"

"I'm not lying! I'm telling the truth!"

"You *do* eat, but only when people can't see you!"

Shelly's teary eyes fell to the ground. Her tears looked real, but she wasn't fooling me. Some bad guys pretended to cry so officers felt sorry for them.

"Miss Walters—"

Jimmy tapped me on the shoulder.

"What is it?"

"Sorry to interrupt, Detective Inspector Dove, but we have a *big* problem..."

He pointed at the teachers coming outside. Mrs Cherry wasn't out yet, but she would be soon. When she blew the whistle, breaktime would be over.

"Miss Walters," I said, "if you're on a no food diet, you won't want *this.*"

I reached into my pocket and pulled out the soggy beef burger Will made earlier.

When I tossed it on to Shelly's lap, her eyes widened and she started drooling. She looked over the burnt beef and squashed bun.

"Go on," I said. "You can have it if you tell the truth. You're fat because you ate all the burgers, isn't it?"

Shelly was drooling so much that spit dripped onto the burger.

"I've got one too," Jimmy said, pulling out a juicy double cheeseburger from his trouser pocket. His burger had tomatoes, lettuce and lots of sloppy ketchup.

Shelly's wide eyes went from my burger to Jimmy's to mine to Jimmy's again.

"Come on, Shelly," Jimmy said. "Just...one...bite."

Mrs Cherry stepped outside with the whistle in her hand. She looked at the other teachers. They all nodded to show they were ready to go inside. Any second now she'd blow the whistle...

Shelly picked up Jimmy's burger and smelt it. Her stomach grumbled really loud. I felt sorry for her poor tummy, but how could it be empty if she was fat? She wasn't really on a diet, was she?

"Take a bite," Jimmy said. "You've done so well on your diet. You deserve a treat!"

Shelly nodded, her stomach growling louder and louder.

Just eat it, I thought. It'll prove you DO eat burgers, not just salad.

"You'd better hurry before it gets colder," Jimmy said.

"It looks so tasty," I said. "Hurry up and eat it before the whistle blows!"

Shelly opened her mouth and slowly brought the burger closer to her lips. Jimmy and I leaned in, waiting for just *one* bite. One bite would make Shelly eat more. If she could eat two MASSIVE, home-made burgers, it would prove she could easily eat ten small, school ones.

"It looks so good," Shelly said. "I haven't had a burger since…Never mind!"

Since stealing the school burgers, I thought. You won't be doing that again!

Suddenly Shelly stopped and turned to Jimmy. She asked, "Do you have any mustard? I like it on my burger."

"No," he said. "Try it without, okay?"

Shelly shrugged and lifted the burger to her mouth again. Then she stopped and put it back down.

"What's wrong now?" I snapped.

"Any extra onions?" she asked. "I love onions!"

"Just eat it," I said. "Now!"

Shelly lifted the burger and looked it over. She smelt it before putting it down again.

"What kind of seasoning did you add?" she asked.

"The ones you like," I said. "Now eat the burgers!"

"But how'd you know which seasoning I like?"

"I asked your friends," I said.

"But I don't have any…"

She looked like she'd cry again, but I knew they were fake tears.

"Eat the burger," I said. "It'll make you feel better."

Slowly Shelly lifted the burger to her lips. She opened her mouth and the burger slid past her teeth. All she had to do was take a bite, but it was too late…

Chapter 14

Mrs Cherry put the whistle to her lips and blew it. Shelly dropped the burger without taking a bite, even though her stomach was growling. She got up and ran to her class. She waved at Jimmy before giving me a mean look.

"What now?" Jimmy asked. "She didn't bite it. Maybe she isn't the burger thief?"

"But she's the fattest person at school. Who else could've eaten all that food?"

"Maybe...maybe...maybe the burger thief *isn't* a fat person?" He got up and brushed dirt off his trousers. "It could be a skinny person like you and me."

"I don't think so," I said. "Maybe Shelly didn't bite the burger because she's got her own burgers at school. She's probably eating them in secret."

"But her stomach is growling like she doesn't eat."

"I think she *does* eat, but not when anybody can see her..."

"What do you mean?" he asked.

"Shelly was seen eating *one* burger. Nurse Mona said so."

"Okay..."

"So where are the other nine?" I pulled him closer so no one heard us talking. "Shelly hid them in school somewhere. She probably eats them when nobody is around."

"Wait a minute," he said. "What if she took the other nine burgers home?"

"No way! Her parents would see them and start asking questions. Then she'd be in big trouble."

We rushed over and joined the line by Mrs Cherry. Jimmy and I kept talking, but lowered our voices.

"Mya, where could Shelly hide nine school burgers?"

"Somewhere very cold," I said. "It'll stop them from going off."

"The school fridge would be a great place to hide food. Maybe the dinner ladies let Shelly hide the burgers in there?"

"But then Shelly couldn't eat them in secret," I said. "The burgers have to be somewhere cold AND quiet. Somewhere cold so the burgers don't go off. Somewhere quiet so no one catches Shelly eating stolen food."

"What's the coldest, quietest room at

school?" he asked.

"The basement," I said. "It's always warmer upstairs than downstairs. That means the basement is the coldest room."

"It's the quietest room, too," Jimmy said. "Nobody's down there much."

Only staff members went into the basement. Students weren't allowed down there because it was too "dangerous". The teachers were scared we'd hurt ourselves on something. That's why no kid had ever been down there.

But the attic was a different story…

I heard that a boy sneaked into the attic and *never* came back down. No one ever saw him again. Eventually everyone forgot his name, what he looked like, and why he went up there.

Very spooky, I thought. I'm glad we're not going up there…

I didn't want to go into the basement either. What if we got caught? Would we get detention or be suspended? Suspended kids were banned from school for weeks!

I felt really sad when I imagined being suspended. Jimmy looked sad too. If he was suspended, he'd be kicked off the football and basketball teams.

"Mya," he whispered, "if we're caught in the basement…"

My perfect school record would be over. Dad would ground me. Mum would take away my badge, my handcuffs and, worst of all, my top secret case files.

Without my police stuff, I'd have to find another job. I could be a nurse like Mum or fix cars like Dad. Or maybe just stay home doing nothing like Will.

No! No! No! I didn't want to be a nurse, a mechanic or a lazy, teenage boy.

I wanted to be a police officer.

Our class went upstairs and everyone sat down. Mrs Cherry started handing out paintbrushes, paint and paper for art class. Usually I'd be very excited about painting, but today I was busy thinking about the police case.

"Are we really going down there?" Jimmy asked. "To the basement?"

"Yeah, sure."

"Aren't you scared of getting caught?"

"Nope. Of course not. Not scared. Not scared at all. Not at all. Nope."

"Are you sure?"

"I'm not scared," I said. "I'm not scared at all..."

Actually, I *was* scared. *Very* scared! I didn't tell Jimmy that, though. As the top police officer on this case, it was my duty to be brave...or at least *pretend* to be brave.

But really, I was scared. Scared of getting kicked out of school. Scared of Mum and Dad finding out. Scared of not being Detective Inspector Mya Dove anymore.

I didn't want to be a nurse, a mechanic or just a student. I wanted to be the best police officer in the entire universe!

"Mya, hello! Anyone home?" Jimmy poked my arm. "I asked you what time we're going into the basement."

"…We're not going down there."

"What?" He almost dropped his paintbrush on the floor. "But Shelly's got to hide the burgers somewhere cold. The basement is the coldest room at school."

"She might've hidden the burgers somewhere else," I said. "We'll look around the playground, the girls' toilets, the boys' toilets, the lunch hall, our classroom and everywhere else but the basement, okay?"

Before he said another word, I turned back to my art work. I tried to have fun painting, but I couldn't enjoy myself.

"Are you okay?" Jimmy asked.

"I'm fine."

I wasn't fine.

All I could think about was the dark, damp, cold basement down below. It was the perfect place to hide nine burgers. Shelly knew it. Jimmy knew it. I knew it. Now we had to go down there and look around, but I was too scared.

And I wasn't just scared of the basement. I was also scared of getting a basement key. We couldn't go down there without it.

Only three people at school had a basement key. We'd have to borrow one of theirs, but which one should we pick?

What if we're caught taking the key? I thought. What if we're caught in the basement?

If Jimmy and I were caught, we'd end up in Mr Badal's office. He'd yell at us for an hour and then call our parents. They'd yell at us too.

If we were *lucky*, we'd just get detention for a month. It might go on our school records.

But if we were *unlucky*, things would be a lot worse. Mr Badal wouldn't just give us a month in detention. He wouldn't just call our angry parents. He wouldn't just ruin our perfect school records. Instead, he'd do something so mean that no student would *ever* take the basement key again.

To scare the other students, Mr Badal would give Jimmy and me the WORST school punishment: expulsion! Anyone expelled was kicked out of school and *never* allowed to come back...

Chapter 15

I couldn't tell Jimmy I was scared to go in the basement. Police officers are supposed to be brave. That's why people come to us when they're scared.

"Are you all right?" Jimmy asked.

"I'm fine," I said. "Everything is just fine."

But it wasn't just fine.

We'd spent our lunch break digging around in bins, looking for the missing burgers. So far all we'd found were rotten fruit, empty water bottles and a football with a hole in it.

I had two more days to prove Shelly stole the burgers and hid them somewhere at school. She'd probably hidden them in the basement, but I was too scared to go down there. That's why I was looking everywhere else for the missing burgers.

"Mya!" Jimmy cried. "Are you listening to me?"

"Did you say something?" I asked. "I didn't hear you right the first time..."

"Yeah, sure," he said with a grin. "I told you I'm ready."

"Ready for what?"

"Ready to go in the basement."

The last basement I'd been in was at Angel's house. We caused so much trouble down there...

"Jimmy, we should keep looking everywhere but the basement," I said. "Shelly could've hidden the burgers anywhere!"

"Mya, we checked the bins, the P.E. cupboard, and even searched the smelly bathrooms."

"I know but—"

"Let's go in the basement, find those burgers, arrest Shelly for stealing, and then eat some crisps." He looked at his watch. "We've only got ten minutes left, but we can do it!"

"No, we still have to check the sandpit, paddling pool, lockers, cupboards in every classroom, the playground—"

"Again?" He crossed his arms. "We've checked every bush, tree and bin out here. Mya, quit stalling! You don't wanna go down there because you're scared!"

"Not true," I snapped. "I'm not scared just smart, that's all."

"...You calling me dumb?"

"No," I said. "If we go down there, we

could get caught!"

"Or maybe you don't want to go down there because..." He grinned and turned away. "Never mind."

"You calling me a chicken?"

"Nope, I'm not saying that…"

I turned him around to face me and held him by the shoulders.

"So what ARE you saying?" I spat. "Say it!"

"You're scared there aren't any burgers down there. It would mean Shelly ISN'T the thief. There might not be any burger thief at all…"

He leaned in so his pointy, white nose was pressing against my round, brown one. He wasn't done talking yet.

"If Shelly isn't the burger thief, it means you spent all week chasing the wrong person *again*!"

I pressed my nose against his. He pressed his nose against mine harder. Soon both our noses were very squashed.

"Poor little Mya," he said. "Five cases in a row. All wrong. After this, you might not get paid. Even worse, you might lose your badge!"

I gasped. Losing my badge would be horrible, but another week without any grapes? Again? No!!!!!!

Mum and Dad hadn't bought me any grapes recently. It was because last month they bought so many I couldn't finish them fast enough. The grapes went mouldy and brown, but that wasn't my fault. If I eat too many at once they make me poo a lot, so I had to eat them slowly each day.

"I can't mess up another case," I said, "but I can't go down there!"

"You're scared."

"Okay, I am, so what?"

"So you *are* scared!" he said. "Well, I can help you with that."

"How?"

"By sharing my dad's favourite quote," he said. "It always makes me feel better when I'm scared."

"I *love* positive quotes," I said. "Tell me your dad's favourite one, please."

"Sure! Here's the quote: It's okay to be scared. Being scared means you're about to do something really, really brave."

"Thanks," I said. "I really needed to hear that."

This whole time I'd been scared of what could go wrong. I thought we'd be caught in the basement and expelled by Mr Badal!

Jimmy's quote reminded me that I was scared AND brave. I was being brave by going into the basement. It was the only way we'd find the burgers and prove Shelly hid them. Then the case would be solved.

When I thought of being brave, I felt happier and started smiling. I wasn't so nervous anymore. Actually, I was excited! Excited about solving the case and stopping the burger thief for good!

"We've only got five minutes left," I said. "Break is over soon!"

Jimmy and I crept inside to the main corridor. We stopped by the basement door, my hands sweaty and shaky.

"We can do this," Jimmy said, pulling me closer to the basement door. "We'll finally catch Shelly...or whoever the burger thief really is!"

He was right. If Shelly wasn't the burger thief, we couldn't just blame everything on her. We'd have to find the real bad guy before more burgers went missing.

If Shelly *was* the burger thief, I had to prove it as soon as possible. In two days, I'd meet my secret boss in the bathroom. She wouldn't be happy if I hadn't solved the case.

"Jimmy," I whispered, "at afternoon breaktime, we're going down there. I promise."

"Really?" Jimmy bounced around. "Cool! I'll be the first ever kid in the basement...Well, at least the first one to come back."

"What do you mean?" I asked. "Who's been down there? Who didn't come back?"

"That boy who went missing years ago. He disappeared in the basement. It's been so long that no one remembers his name, face or anything else about him."

"I thought the boy went missing in the spooky attic!"

"Nope. The spooky basement." Jimmy

pulled me closer. "You can hear him scream if you're really quiet..."

I heard something coming from behind the door. Was it a scream? No. Was it a shout? No. Or was it a growl? Yes! But it wasn't coming from behind the door. It was coming from my stomach. I was really hungry! Now I knew how Shelly felt on her no food diet.

"Jimmy, if that boy is still down there, he might be angry and want to hurt us."

"Why would he be angry?"

"When we show up, he'll think that we came to save him," I said. "Soon he'll realise we're saving the burgers, not him. He won't be happy about that..."

"Don't worry about him, okay? I'll keep you safe." He took my hand and squeezed it, making my cheeks feel warm. "Anyway, how could he stay down there for so long?"

"He might be eating school burgers with Shelly. That could be how he's managed without shopping for food."

"If he's been down there for years, we're gonna see some gross stuff," he said. "The basement must be full of rubbish and lots of junk because he can't throw anything out."

I held my nose and Jimmy laughed.

"So, are we going down there after French?" he asked.

"Yep, but there's a problem…" I turned the door handle. The basement door stayed shut. "It's locked."

Adults always locked doors they didn't want us opening.

"We need a basement key," I said.

"Uh oh…"

There were three basement keys. The school only trusted three people with them: Mr Badal (the headteacher), Mrs Cherry (the deputy headteacher), and Mr Murphy (the caretaker).

"Jimmy, we need a basement key, but they won't just hand one over."

"So we're *borrowing* a basement key and then putting it back before we get caught? Sounds like a good plan to me!"

"Thanks," I said. "Now let's get moving!"

We headed back outside to get away from the basement door. We couldn't be seen next to it or a teacher might figure out what we were planning. Then our top secret case wouldn't be a secret anymore.

Keeping secrets is very important when you're working on a case. If top secret work gets out, the bad guys will know what you're planning and run away. Then you might *never* catch them!

"Whose basement key should we borrow?" I asked Jimmy. "Mr Badal, Mrs Cherry or Mr

Murphy's?"

Jimmy gulped when I said Mr Badal's name.

"Can we try to get Mrs Cherry's key?" he asked. "If we're caught by her, we'll just get some detention. Getting caught by Mr Badal would be much, much worse…"

"What about Mr Murphy?" I asked. "I spoke to him the other day and he was really nice and helpful. Maybe we could get a basement key from him?"

"He won't just give us the key," Jimmy said. "How can we get it?"

I stopped to think over some ideas. It took a minute or so, but I finally had a plan that might work.

"I'll keep Mr Murphy busy while you sneak in. Grab the key and get out. Easy, right?"

"Sorry but I need more info than that," he

said. "I've got some questions."

"Go on," I said. "We've got time."

"Okay…You said you'll keep Mr Murphy busy, but how will you do that? How long will you keep him busy for? What if he spots me sneaking around? What if he figures out our plan? Do we have a Plan B, Plan C, Plan D and Plan E?"

"Don't worry about all that," I said. "I'll keep him talking so he won't see you. Just focus on getting that basement key!"

Jimmy had asked me so many questions, but I didn't listen to him. If I'd listened, we would've had a great plan and organised everything step-by-step.

We also would've thought of a back-up plan, just in case things went wrong. All that planning would've made things much easier.

But I didn't listen to Jimmy. I ignored his questions. That's why things were about to go horribly wrong...

Chapter 16

At afternoon breaktime, Jimmy and I crept down the back staircase. We stopped outside Mr Murphy the caretaker's room. We needed his basement key, but he wouldn't just hand it over. That's why we needed a distraction.

I was the distraction.

I was going to talk to Mr Murphy while Jimmy sneaked into the room. We agreed that if he got caught, we'd act like we didn't know each other. That meant I wouldn't be in trouble too.

"Are you ready?" Jimmy asked.

"Let's do this," I said, my heart racing.

Jimmy dashed down the corridor and slipped into the boys' toilets. He held the bathroom door open a tiny crack so he could look outside without being seen.

After a long, deep breath to calm myself down, I knocked on Mr Murphy's door.

"Who is it?" Mr Murphy yelled.

"It's me!"

"Who's *me*?"

"Mr Murphy."

"No, who's YOU? Who are *you*?"

"Detective Inspector Mya Dove," I replied. "Could you open up, please?"

"I'm doing lots of important, um, work in here," he said. "What do you want?"

"I'm here to talk about…"

My mind went blank. I was supposed to say something to make him come out, but I couldn't remember what.

"You still there, Inspector?" he asked.

"Yes. Just a minute, please!"

I closed my eyes and remembered the last time I'd spoken to him. He'd said the burger thief was probably a squirrel.

"I don't know if you remember me, Mr Murphy, but we talked outside Mrs Cherry's classroom. I'm the girl who bumped her head."

"Hope you're feeling better," he said. "We had a nice chat, but I can't talk right now. I have an important, uh, meeting."

"I have something very important to tell you," I said. "Remember when you said squirrels were stealing our burgers?"

"No one believes me..."

"They will now," I said. "I have proof."

The door flew open and Mr Murphy stepped outside, grinning from ear to ear.

"I knew it! I knew it," he cried. "Those

grey squirrels stole our burgers."

"I have proof outside in the playground. Come see, Mr Murphy."

He glanced back and shook his head.

"I can't go, little one," he said. "My very important, um, thing starts soon…"

"The match is starting soon!" a man yelled. "The players are coming out."

"I thought you had an important meeting, Sir…"

"That's the TV," he said, blushing. "The footie is on at the moment. It's half time."

Football was very popular in England. There were so many matches that it was hard to keep up with who was playing who. That's why I preferred tennis. It was much easier to understand.

"Please come outside!"

"Maybe later."

"But my squirrel proof is outside," I said.

"Come quickly or the squirrels might hide it. Then we won't be able to prove they took our burgers!"

A loud whistle blew. I covered my ears and looked through the doorway. On the TV were players kicking the ball about.

"I'm busy right now, kid," he said. "Go play outside with your friends."

He started to close the door, so I pushed it back open and stepped past him.

"You're not allowed in here, kid!"

"This is a nice place you've got," I said, walking around the small room. "All these places to HIDE, I mean keep stuff."

I hoped Jimmy had heard me. We only had twelve minutes left before break was over. We couldn't try again the next day because Mr Murphy would be suspicious.

"You like what I did with the place?" he asked. "My wife said it's a bit messy."

His wife was right.

In a corner of the room was a wonky two-seater sofa with cushions thrown on it. Beside it was a stained coffee table covered in old, torn magazines. Pressed against the wall was a rusty, metal stand with a small TV on it. That small TV made a lot of noise!

The rest of the room was full of cardboard boxes, plastic containers and toolboxes. They were stacked against the walls. The boxes weren't closed properly, so things were spilling out. Anything that fell on the floor was left there, making it hard to walk around.

Everywhere I looked were hammers, drills, screwdrivers, nails, rulers, blocks of wood, the school's floorplans and cans of white paint. The white shade matched the paint on every ceiling and wall at school.

Next to the door was a square, silver box on the wall. There was a key sitting in the lock.

"What's in there?" I asked. When I reached out to turn the key, he wagged his finger at me.

"In there are fifty school keys. No students, not even Prefects, are allowed to touch them."

"ALL the school keys are in there?" I asked. "Even keys to the nursery gate, the attic, the basement?"

When I said the word basement, Mr Murphy's face turned pale. His fuzzy, black moustache twitched and his eyes moved back to the TV.

"The basement is horrible," he said. "That's why no kids, not even Prefects, are allowed down there."

"What's so horrible about the school basement?" I asked.

"Anyway, time for you to go!"

He tried to wave me outside but I didn't move.

"Is there something else you wanted, kid?" he grumbled. "I'm missing the game, you know?"

Thoughts raced around my mind like sports cars on a track. Every time I thought of something to say, I thought of reasons not to say it. Ideas were good one second and bad the next. With time ticking away, I couldn't stand around doing nothing.

Don't be afraid to do something, Mum would say. You'll never know unless you try.

I wanted to know what was in the basement. I wanted to know if Shelly was the burger thief. But I'd never know unless I got that basement key.

What could I say to get Mr Murphy to leave his room? I thought. What would be more important to him than football?

Once again, I remembered our talk from the other day. He'd mentioned a big poo someone left in the bathroom. He wasn't happy about it, and I could see why. I wouldn't like to clean a dirty toilet either. At home, Mum always did it for us.

"Mr Murphy, I told a fib earlier," I said. "I don't have proof that squirrels took the missing burgers."

Mr Murphy crossed his arms and looked down his pointy, pink nose at me.

"So, kid, why're you wasting your break AND making me miss the game?"

"Because I wanted you to go upstairs to the girls' bathroom," I said. "I heard some girls talking in the playground and...Never mind! I shouldn't tell on people!"

"If someone's been naughty, tell on 'em! Go on!"

"Well, I shouldn't be telling you this, but

a Year Six girl said she needed to poo really badly. She said she hasn't been in weeks!"

"Weeks? That can't be healthy..."

"It's been in there for a while," I said. "When it finally comes out...Whoa! I feel sorry for the cleaners!"

"What about *me*?" he cried. "The cleaners only tidy up afterwards. I'm the one who has to unblock that monster in the toilet!"

"It's gonna be bad," I said. "She's been eating lots and lots of curry and beans."

"The little terror! It took me an hour to clear a toilet backlog the other day. The thing was the size of a tree trunk!"

He stormed out of the room and marched towards the staircase. Because of his heavy footsteps, he didn't hear Jimmy running from the boys' toilets to the caretaker's room.

Now all I had to do was keep Mr Murphy upstairs. While we were upstairs, Jimmy could get the basement key from the silver key box. He'd run back to the toilets before Mr Murphy and I returned.

That's what I thought would happen but...

"Darn it!" Mr Murphy cried. "You wait here. I need to go back."

Oh no, I thought. He's gonna catch Jimmy!

I ran ahead of Mr Murphy and stopped in front of his room. I spread my arms wide and planted my feet to the floor.

"We've got to go upstairs and stop the smelly poop," I cried. "My nose is counting on you."

"Kid, that little terror won't get away with this," he said, "but I forgot to do something. We can go in a second, all right?"

"But—"

He squeezed past me and went to the sofa.

I looked out the corner of my eye. There was a shadowy figure peeking out from behind the boxes.

"I found 'em!" Mr Murphy pulled out a bunch of keys from behind the sofa cushions. "I never leave without 'em."

The keys in the box by the door were back-up keys. Good. As long as Mr Murphy had the main keys, he wouldn't notice that any back-up keys were missing.

I walked out, but when I looked back Mr Murphy was fumbling over his keys.

"What's wrong?" I asked.

"Found it," he said, holding up a dirty key. "Gimme a second, kid."

"A second for what?"

I watched in horror as Mr Murphy shoved the key into the door and locked it.

Click!

Just like that, poor Jimmy was locked in

Mr Murphy's room. There was no other way out. No other door or any windows.

Jimmy was trapped!

Mr Murphy would come back soon. He'd find Jimmy hiding behind the boxes. Jimmy would be told off, and things would be even worse if he'd taken the basement key.

"If I get caught, pretend you don't know me," Jimmy said earlier. "There's no point in us both getting into trouble."

He was right. If we were both told off then we'd both get detention. If we both got detention then we'd both lose our police badges. The bad guys would be very happy when they found out that two of the best police officers had lost their jobs.

"Pretend you don't know me…" his voice echoed in my head. How could I? Jimmy was my friend. He'd been there for me so many times. Could I just leave him alone?

When Mr Murphy caught him in the caretaker's room, all I had to do was pretend I didn't know him. Just look the other way and act like we weren't friends.

But I felt guilty about letting Jimmy take all the blame. How could I be happy with my badge knowing he'd lost his?

"Let's go, Detective!" Mr Murphy said happily. "Lead the way!"

When we went upstairs, I thought long and hard about what to do next. I had two choices: save Jimmy or save myself.

If I saved Jimmy, he wouldn't lose his badge or get detention, but helping him wouldn't be easy. I might get caught. Then we'd both be in big trouble. That meant the case wouldn't be solved, and the burger thief wouldn't be stopped.

What's more important? I thought. Saving Jimmy or solving the case?

Or could I do both...?

Chapter 17

Mr Murphy's face was dark red when we reached the girls' bathroom. After I made sure the toilets were empty, he stormed inside and reached for the closest toilet brush.

"Do you know which toilet she was in?" he asked. "I'll need to assess the mess immediately."

"I'm not sure. She said she was going to do a really big one upstairs and that she hoped it would block the drains."

"She sounds like a troublesome child." He sniffed a little. "It doesn't smell like she dropped a big one, but I won't know until I get a closer look."

Mr Murphy went into each toilet stall and slowly edged towards the toilet. He gripped the toilet brush tightly in one hand while the other hand pinched his nose.

"Nothing in here," he said. "Let's try the next one." There was nothing in there either. Or the next one. Or the toilet after that.

When all ten toilets had been checked, he marched out with an angry look on his face.

"Kid, are you sure this girl was pooing in here?" He glared at me, tapping his foot. "Doesn't smell or look like anyone—"

The bell rang. Oh no! Jimmy and I were out of time...

"Never mind," he said. "Just go outside and line up. Your teacher will be waiting."

"What about you?"

"I'm going back to the footie. I hope

they've scored!"

In a minute or so, Mr Murphy would catch Jimmy in the caretaker's room. He didn't know Jimmy was my friend, so I wouldn't be in trouble. I could go outside and line up while Jimmy took all the blame.

But that wasn't the right thing to do.

Jimmy and I were a team. I couldn't just leave him behind. I had to find a way to help him!

"I can't go outside right now," I said, my thoughts racing. "I, um, left my pen in your room."

"I'll bring it to your classroom later. Mrs Cherry is your teacher, yes?"

"I need the pen for class," I said. "I don't have another blue pen, just a pink one. I can't do my work in pink, you know?"

Mr Murphy sighed heavily. He dumped the toilet brush in the cleaning cupboard and we headed back downstairs.

When we reached his door, I knocked on it loudly and shouted, "Blue pen, I'm back! Don't you think of hiding near the sofa or TV. That's where we'll be looking!"

"Kid, has anyone told you you're a bit odd?" He turned the key and pushed open the door. "Kids these days. It must be something in those fizzy drinks."

Before Mr Murphy could go inside, I pushed past him and pretended to look for my lost pen.

"Where'd you last see it?" Mr Murphy asked. "What's it look like?"

"It looks like a normal pen with a blue tip."

"I've got loads lying around," he said. "You could take one of mine."

"No thanks! That pen is my favourite. I want it back."

"Okay, kid, whatever…"

Mr Murphy seemed more interested in the football match than looking for my pen.

"It might've rolled under the sofa," I said. "Can you check for me, please?"

"But the match—"

"Please, Sir!" I cried. "The whistle's gone and class is starting soon!"

Lots of footsteps were marching down the corridor. Our class was waiting for their turn to come inside.

Mr Murphy huffed and got on the floor. He peered under the sofa and squinted, trying to see in the shadows.

"I need my torch," he said. "It's by my toolbox."

Which toolbox? He had loads on the messier side of the room.

Mr Murphy stood up and headed straight for the toolboxes. I spotted Jimmy peeking out from behind them. If Mr Murphy went over there, he'd see Jimmy. I had to do something!

"I'll get the toolbox," I said, rushing ahead of him.

"You don't know which toolbox I'm talking about." He stepped around me and kept walking.

Suddenly Mr Murphy stopped and turned back.

"What's wrong?" I asked.

"I think it's been *opened*."

"What's been opened, Sir?"

"The key box."

Slowly he moved to the silver box on the wall. He opened it and stared at the keys inside.

"Someone touched my keys," he said. "Nothing is missing but...the lunch room key is back to front. I always make sure the ridges face the right side, not the left."

I didn't have time to ask what ridges were or why he liked them facing the right.

"Nobody touched your keys, Sir." I laughed nervously. "You locked the door. No one's been in here but us."

"You sure about that?" he said. "This place is much bigger than it looks. My stuff makes it seem smaller, but there's lots of space to hide over there."

He pointed at the toolboxes where Jimmy had hidden earlier.

"I know you're there," Mr Murphy barked. "Come out right now!"

I couldn't see Jimmy moving in the darkness.

"Fine then, little man," Mr Murphy said. "If you won't come out, I'm going in…"

Chapter 18

Mr Murphy pulled out a walkie talkie from his pocket and held it to his mouth.

"Mandy, please get a detention chair ready," he told the school receptionist. "We've got a very naughty boy here."

Mandy didn't say anything back. I'd never seen her ignore someone before. She was always the nicest, kindest, sweetest person at school.

Wait a minute, I thought. Something's not right here…

My walkie talkie had a light that changed

from red (Off) to green (On). The light on Mr Murphy's walkie talkie was red.

My walkie talkie crackled when I used it. Mr Murphy's walkie talkie didn't make any noise at all.

The red light and silence meant the walkie talkie wasn't on!

He's pretending to use the walkie talkie, I thought. Jimmy, don't fall for it!

Mr Murphy was trying to trick Jimmy into coming out. It wasn't working, though. Jimmy stayed in the darkness.

"Kid, you've got ONE more chance to come out."

That meant I had one more chance to save Jimmy.

What should I do? I thought. I've got to stop Mr Murphy from going over there!

"Detective, go to class," Mr Murphy said, opening the door. "I'll make sure this naughty boy goes straight to Mr Badal!"

Mr Murphy crept closer and closer to Jimmy's hiding spot. He'd catch him really, really soon.

What should I do? I thought again. Maybe I should follow our plan!

All I had to do was follow our original plan. I was supposed to distract Mr Murphy while Jimmy sneaked in and out. Mr Murphy messed everything up when he locked the door.

If I distracted Mr Murphy again, Jimmy could sneak out. I needed a very big distraction to keep Mr Murphy busy! Then Jimmy would have enough time to escape.

What would be a very big distraction? I thought. Aha! I know...

I rushed into the corridor and cried, "A rat! I saw a rat!"

The girls started screaming and ran

around. Some of the boys ran after them while others stayed behind, looking for the rat.

Teachers came out of classrooms, trying to calm down the screaming girls. The cleaners appeared with mops and brooms. They banged them against the radiators and walls, trying to scare the rat out of its hiding place.

Mr Murphy rushed out and stopped beside me.

"What's going on?" he asked.

"Someone saw a rat," I said.

"Where'd it go?" he asked, looking up and down the corridor.

"I think it went to the nursery," I said. "I heard the rat was as big as a cat."

"Just like last time," he muttered. He turned back to his room and glared at the darkness. I imagined Jimmy glaring right back. "It's your lucky day, kid!"

Mr Murphy rushed into the corridor and squeezed through the people running by. He got on his hands and knees and crawled about. He kept stopping to check any holes and gaps in the walls.

I slipped back into the caretaker's room and waved at Jimmy. He peeked out.

Suddenly Mr Murphy's heavy footsteps sounded closer and closer. Was he coming back?

No. He rushed past me and didn't stop until he reached Mr Badal's office.

"Jimmy, let's go!"

Jimmy ran from his hiding place and grabbed my hand. Together we rushed down the corridor.

"We're gonna be late!" I cried.

"We've still got time! Run!"

When we got upstairs, we started running towards our classroom. Mrs Cherry's back was facing the corridor. Soon she'd unpack her things and close the door. Anyone who came after that would be marked as late.

"Run," Jimmy huffed. "Run! Run! Run!"

I was running as fast as I could but Jimmy was way ahead of me. He reached the classroom and stopped running just before Mrs Cherry turned around.

She saw me.

"Mya," Mrs Cherry said, "slow down or you'll hurt yourself again."

She left the door open and started writing on the board.

When I walked into the classroom, everyone looked very surprised. Usually, late people were told off, but not me. Probably because I'd tripped over and hurt myself the other day.

"Teacher's pet," Angel grumbled, her white face going red. "She should get detention for being late twice!"

I didn't say anything to her. She wasn't worth getting into trouble over. Instead of arguing with her, I held my head high and walked right past her.

I sat at my desk and took a deep breath. We hadn't got the basement key, but we hadn't been caught either.

"You okay?" Jimmy whispered.

"We didn't get the key," I said. "What do we do now?"

"Only three people have a basement key: Mr Badal, Mr Murphy and Mrs Cherry."

"You could've been caught by Mr Murphy," I said. "What if it was Mr Badal instead? Mr Murphy wanted you in detention. Mr Badal would've kicked you out of school!"

Jimmy's eyes widened in fear. We both knew Mr Badal liked him, but not enough to hand over the basement key.

"So that leaves Mrs Cherry then," he said. "We need her basement key."

We also needed more time.

It was Wednesday afternoon. There weren't any more breaktimes that day. We'd have to search the basement on Thursday.

"We'll get Mrs Cherry's basement key tomorrow," I said. "And, um…"

"What?"

"I just wanted to say you were right earlier."

"Right about what?"

"About planning properly," I said. "If I'd listened to you, we might've had Mr Murphy's basement key."

"I know," he said. "Anyway, it's too late now. Let's make the plan better for next time, okay?"

"How could it be better?" I asked.

"Last time, you distracted Mr Murphy while I tried to borrow the key," he said. "This time I'll do the distracting and you'll borrow the key."

"Me?"

"Yes," he said. "Tomorrow I'll keep Mrs Cherry very, very busy. It'll give you time to get the basement key from her desk."

"We'll do it at morning breaktime," I said. "Mrs Cherry will be the only one in class. It'll be easy to distract her and take the key."

"We can't take the basement key in the morning," he said. "If she needs it later, she'll realise it's gone missing. We'll borrow it in the afternoon instead."

"If we can't take the key at morning breaktime, what about lunchtime or afternoon breaktime?"

"We can't take the basement key at *any* breaktime."

"Why not?" I asked.

"If the key goes missing when it's just you, me and Mrs Cherry around, she'll know we took it. It'll be obvious!"

"But we can't take it when other people are around. They'll see me with the key!"

"Not if you're very, very careful," he said. "I'll keep Mrs Cherry and everyone else busy, okay?"

"Everyone else? Wait a minute…"

I realised what his plan was.

"You guessed it," he said. "I'll keep Mrs Cherry busy while you snatch the key at class time."

Just thinking about the basement key made me nervous. I couldn't take it when our class was there. They'd see me!

"I'm not doing it."

"Then you're not solving the case," he said. "Another officer will do it instead."

If someone else solved my case, they'd get *my* reward. I didn't want anyone taking my juicy, green grapes!

"Fine, I'll do it," I said. "Just make sure you keep everyone distracted, okay?"

"Don't worry," he said. "I know just what to do..."

Chapter 19

Today we'd finally go into the basement. To get down there, we needed a basement key. Trying to get one from Mr Murphy had gone very wrong! I hoped that getting Mrs Cherry's key would be easier.

Mrs Cherry stuck a world map on the whiteboard and sat at her desk. On the desk were her keys. The black one was the basement key. Everyone knew that. That's why we never looked at it, let alone touched it.

"Class, please continue the geography

work we started last lesson. If you get stuck, let me know."

Usually Mrs Cherry walked around class while we worked. She'd ask some questions and check our answers.

Sometimes she caught people being naughty. One Monday morning, a girl was caught playing with her phone under the desk. Mrs Cherry took it away and didn't give it back until Friday afternoon.

"Are you ready, Mya?" Jimmy asked.

I nodded.

"Wait for Mrs Cherry to start walking around," he whispered. "When she's talking to someone, get to her desk and wait for my distraction. Grab the key when everyone's looking at me!"

I grabbed a pencil from my pencil case and broke the tip off. Now I could use Mrs Cherry's pencil sharpener. It was on the desk near the keys.

"She'll get up any minute now," Jimmy said. "Wait for it!"

I waited.

And waited.

And waited…

Tick tock, tick tock. Ten minutes went by, but Mrs Cherry stayed at her desk.

"I can't take the basement key if she's sitting at her desk," I whispered. "Why isn't she getting up? Why won't she walk around?"

"I don't know!"

Why didn't Mrs Cherry walk around to check on everyone? Instead, she leaned over and opened her handbag. She sighed before pulling out a very bulky plastic bag.

"Oh no," Jimmy whispered. "That looks like…"

"Not now," I said. "She can't do this now! Not today!"

"What should we do?"

"Let's wait and see," I said. "We could be wrong."

When Mrs Cherry opened the plastic bag, our nightmare came true: she'd brought exam papers. They were thick papers, probably for Year Six.

Year Six exams were really tough. If the older kids didn't do well, it made the whole school look bad. That's why they had so many hard practice papers. Unfortunately, it was Mrs Cherry's turn to mark them.

This was bad news.

She'd be so busy marking exam papers that she'd stay at her desk for the whole lesson. That meant I couldn't grab the basement key and solve the case.

"She's not gonna get up now," I whispered. "Those papers look huge. She'll be marking them forever and ever!"

"I've got a back-up plan," Jimmy said. "I'll keep her busy while you get the key."

"You sure?" I asked. "If you want to back out, now's the time."

"No way! This is too much fun!"

At least *he* was having fun. I definitely wasn't. My heart was racing so fast it was scary!

Could I really take the key from Mrs Cherry's desk? What if someone saw me? Would they tell on me? I knew Angel and her mean friends definitely would!

"Mya," Jimmy whispered, "you done your work yet?"

We had to match each city with the right country.

"Lagos is in...Nigeria," I told myself, circling Nigeria. "Accra is in…Ghana."

I quickly answered each question on the worksheet. Then I double checked my answers twice and turned my sheet over.

Jimmy waved at Mrs Cherry. She looked happy to stop marking the exam papers. Marking them looked boring, but I bet it was more fun than sitting the exam.

"Yes, Jimmy?" Mrs Cherry asked.

"Miss, I wrote a poem about the world. May I recite it?"

"Recite? My goodness, Jimmy, your vocabulary is impressive!" Mrs Cherry leaned back in her desk chair. "Come over to the whiteboard, please."

"May I recite it from my desk?" He stood up and pushed out his chair. "Could you listen from here, next to me? You deserve a break from those exam papers."

"Well, I just started working but...I'd like a break," she said, rushing over. "Regular breaks keep the mind fresh!"

When she came over, I showed her the

broken pencil tip. She nodded, so I hurried over to the pencil sharpener on her desk.

Being so close to the basement key made me nervous. I felt like everyone was watching me, but they weren't when I checked. They were still stuck on those hard questions at the end.

I started sharpening very slowly, keeping my eyes on Angel and her friends. They were copying each other's answers, which is obviously cheating. Usually I'd tell on them, but not today. I couldn't tell Mrs Cherry they were being naughty when I was being naughty myself.

All I had to do was knock the keys into the bin. Then I'd reach inside and pull off the basement key without anyone noticing. Afterwards, I'd put the other keys back on the desk.

"Go on, Jimmy," Mrs Cherry said. "Recite

your masterpiece!"

"I call this poem….Geography!"

Mrs Cherry clapped.

"Today Miss is teaching us geography. The whole wide world is full of sea."

He paused.

"We're matching the right country to the right city. If we get it wrong, it's such a pity."

I moved closer to the keys. I glanced over at Angel, who was still busy cheating. Good. At least she wasn't looking at me.

Jimmy continued.

"Seven continents around the world. One for every boy and girl."

"That's silly," Angel cried. "There are seven continents and seven *billion* people. There are not enough continents for every boy and girl!"

"Silence, Angel!" Mrs Cherry snapped. "How rude to interrupt such a lovely, heartfelt poem. Apologise this instant!"

"Sorry," Angel grumbled. She turned to me and glared.

"How long does it take to sharpen one pencil?" Angel asked. "What are you doing over there?"

I sharpened faster, snapping the tip on purpose.

"Take time, Mya," Mrs Cherry said. "Don't let people rush you like that. Just take time and do things properly."

I started sharpening again, very, very slowly.

Jimmy continued.

"All that ocean and all that sea. All the fish and crabs are free."

I moved closer to Mrs Cherry's keys. It was a big bunch of keys, so she wouldn't miss one right away. Not with all those papers to mark.

But Angel was still watching me very closely. Her eyes moved from the desk to me and back to the desk. Soon she'd figure out what was going on.

You don't have much time, I thought to myself. Just go for it!

I sat on the desk and pretended to bump the keys off with my hip. They fell over the side but missed the bin and landed on the floor.

"What was that?" Mrs Cherry asked.

The other students looked under their desks.

"Mya, what's going on?" Mrs Cherry asked.

"I just—"

Jimmy blew his nose so loudly that Mrs Cherry covered her ears. He rubbed his eyes, leaving them puffy and pink. It looked like he was going to cry.

"Miss, I don't think anyone is listening," Jimmy said, pulling a sad face. "I knew my poem was bad. I won't bother finishing it. Sorry I disturbed you all…"

"Jimmy, you didn't disturb anyone!" Mrs Cherry ordered everyone to turn around. "We're still listening to your marvellous work. I'm very proud of you."

Jimmy smiled.

When everyone turned away, I grabbed the keys. I pulled the basement key off and shoved it into my pocket.

Quickly, I returned the other keys to the desk. It was easier now that everyone was looking at Jimmy. Even Angel wasn't watching me anymore. She was too busy laughing at Jimmy's poem with her friends.

I returned to my desk.

Holding the cold, hard basement key made me realise what we were about to do.

Was I really going into the dark, scary basement? Was I about to catch Shelly the burger thief? And if Shelly *wasn't* the burger thief, who else could it be…?

Chapter 20

After a long geography lesson, the bell finally rang. This was it. We were going into the basement. My legs felt wobbly because of nerves and excitement.

"You ready, Mya?" Jimmy asked.

"I think so."

Jimmy and I followed our class out and headed for the stairs. We acted like it was a normal Thursday afternoon so no one figured out our big secret.

I slipped my hand into my trouser pocket and wrapped my fingers around the basement key. I felt so powerful holding it! If other students knew it was there, they would've tried to take it.

Or maybe they wouldn't because the basement was dangerous. A boy had gone missing down there. He hadn't been seen since…

He could still be down there, hiding in the shadows. Watching. Waiting. Ready to get revenge because no one went looking for him.

If anyone left me in a dark, damp basement for years, I'd be very angry too. Would the boy be angry at us? I hoped not. It wasn't our fault that his friends left him down there.

"Mya, we're almost there," Jimmy whispered, his voice shakier than my legs. His hands were trembling when we reached the stairs, so he shoved them into his pockets.

It's a bad idea to walk with your hands in your pockets. If you trip over, your hands can't break your fall. You might end up landing on your face like I did the other day.

"Jimmy, hands out of your pockets," Mrs Cherry said.

"Sorry, Sir...I mean *Miss*!"

Jimmy wiped his sweaty face on his sleeve. More and more sweat trickled down as we got closer to the basement door.

We couldn't stop by the door because Mrs Cherry was nearby. If she saw us outside the basement, she might figure out our secret. For now, we had no choice but to go outside with everyone else.

Outside, Jimmy and I stayed near the door so we could see through its glass panels. It was a great way to keep an eye on the downstairs corridor. When it was empty, we could sneak in and open the basement door.

"Wait for the teachers to go," Jimmy said. "We'll be in the basement real soon!"

Instead of going to the staff room, Mrs Cherry started chatting to Mrs Tipple, the Year Five teacher. They talked about textbooks and exam papers. Then they talked about the school pet and school trips. Then they talked about…

"If they don't go soon, we'll run out of time," I said.

"I'm sure they'll go in a minute," Jimmy said. "Well, I hope so…"

Two more teachers stopped to chat. They all turned away from the door, whispering to each other. Mrs Cherry glanced at the basement door and started whispering again.

"I think they're talking about the basement," I whispered. "They might know about the boy down there. Maybe they're scared of him too…"

Mr Murphy appeared, carrying two small cardboard boxes. He stopped by the basement door and reached for his keys.

"I'll open it for you," Mrs Cherry said, reaching for her keys.

Oh no, I thought. She'll know her basement key is missing!

"It's all right, I've got it," Mr Murphy said. "It's breaktime, remember? Relax!"

They smiled at each other before he went inside. Now the teachers looked very excited, making me wonder what was in those boxes.

"We can't search the basement if Mr Murphy is down there," I said. "We can't go inside because the teachers are there. Everything's going wrong!"

Jimmy's narrow eyes moved around the playground. He was thinking of a plan, but what?

"Sometimes teachers stay in the corridor

all breaktime," he said. "They'll only move if they HAVE to."

"When would a teacher HAVE to leave the corridor?" I asked. "When the fire alarm goes off, I guess, but we can't set them off. They're only for emergencies."

"What if Mr Badal called them for a very, very important meeting? They'd be too scared not to go!"

"How can we make him do that?"

"We can't," he said. "No one makes Mr Badal do anything he doesn't want to. Got any other ideas?"

"Only one but…but…but we can't do it. It would be too naughty!"

"Tell me."

"Mr Murphy and the teachers would come out if a fight started. But we can't do something like that. People would get hurt."

"Only if it was a REAL fight…"

Jimmy waved at his friends on the football pitch. Two boys stopped and looked at us. Jimmy held up three fingers and the boys nodded.

The first boy ran down the pitch and picked up the football.

"Handball!" the second boy cried. "We get a free kick!"

"No way," the first boy shouted. "I wanna play basketball instead."

"It's a football, not a basketball! Put it down and kick it!"

The first boy started bouncing the football up and down. He pointed at the second boy and started laughing.

A big argument broke out.

"It's all fake," Jimmy said. "They've been friends since nursery."

There was no punching or kicking, only really loud yelling, but their fight was still scary. If I didn't know better, I would've thought the fight was real.

Soon the whole playground ran to the pitch. Half the kids cheered for the first boy and half cheered for the second.

The teachers rushed outside.

"What's going on?" Mrs Cherry asked us. "Did you see what happened?"

"A fight," Jimmy said. "You'd better get over there, Miss!"

When the teachers heard that, they knew there was trouble. Big trouble. Mrs Cherry blew her whistle and ran to the pitch. The other teachers followed behind.

But Mr Murphy wasn't there.

"Maybe he went to get Mr Badal when the fight started," Jimmy said.

"What if he's still down there?" I asked as we walked inside.

"Then we'll sneak past him."

We stopped by the basement door. I took the key out of my pocket and shoved it into the lock. I turned slowly until I heard a loud click.

The door opened a crack, making a squeaky noise. We looked over our shoulders. Luckily no one else was there, but we had to hurry. The fake fight outside wouldn't last long now the teachers were there.

"We're going into the basement," I said. "Are you ready?"

Jimmy turned bright pink, sweat dripping down his face. He didn't answer me. All he could do was nod, his eyes on the basement door.

"Let's do this," I said. "Basement, here we come!"

"Wait!" Jimmy cried.

"Why? What's wrong?" I looked over my shoulder. "Is someone coming?"

"No, me first," Jimmy said, pushing past me. He put one foot through the basement doorway and smiled. "The first kid to ever step into the basement. The other boy doesn't count because he never came back."

I would've liked to be first...

"Mya, I'm gonna tell my friends about this!" He pulled his foot back. "Okay, after you. Girls first."

"You mean *ladies* first."

Because I was a *lady*, I walked in first. Sure, it took a few seconds to actually go in but what can I say? I was still really nervous.

When I walked through the basement doorway, I imagined what would happen next...

I pictured a long, dark staircase leading down to a pitch-black door. The door would lead to a spooky basement, just like in the horror movies Will watched.

The creepy basement would be full of junk everyone had forgotten about, like broken toys, an old computer, and a smelly sock with a hole in it.

I imagined us following a trail of burger wrappers to a growling noise in the shadows. A moment later, we'd find Shelly gobbling down nine burgers!

"You got me," she'd say. "Or not!"

Shelly would run away, but because fat people don't exercise, she'd get tired and stop for a break. That's when Jimmy would jump on her and tickle her stomach. While she was giggling, I'd put handcuffs on her and take her upstairs. We'd go straight to Mr Badal's office, where Shelly would finally tell the truth.

"I'm the burger thief!" she'd say. "I stole the burgers because I'm fat,"

That's what I thought would happen, but

I forgot that things don't always go to plan...

Chapter 21

"Jimmy, are you sure this is the right way?" I asked. "Is the spooky, creepy basement really down…*there*?"

Jimmy shrugged, a confused look on his face.

We'd expected a long, dark staircase leading down to a scary basement. Instead we found a short, bright corridor leading to a shiny elevator.

We hurried to the elevator and pressed the button. The doors slid open. It was huge inside with enough space for my bed, bedside table and wardrobe!

"Let's go down," Jimmy said.

There were two silver, elevator buttons with GROUND FLOOR on one and BASEMENT on the other.

We pushed the BASEMENT button.

The doors closed.

No going back now, I thought. This is it!

The basement was only one floor down, so it didn't take long to reach it. But when the elevator stopped, the doors didn't open. Were we trapped? What was happening?

"Jimmy, let's go back up," I whispered. "I think we broke the elevator."

Jimmy pressed his ear against the doors and put a finger to his lips.

"Can you hear that?" he asked.

At first, all I heard was us breathing. Then I heard different voices and sounds like someone was changing TV channels. Why would a television be in a damp, dark basement?

"I can hear a TV," I said.

"Me too. You know what I *can't* hear?" Jimmy pointed upstairs. "The fake fight."

He was right. I couldn't hear anyone shouting or yelling.

The whistle blew! Mrs Cherry had ended playtime early because of the fight. Soon everyone would come back inside.

Now I was REALLY scared. I couldn't remember if we'd closed the basement door behind us. What if the teachers called the elevator back up? They'd find us inside!

The TV noise turned down. Now I could hear keys jangling outside the elevator door. Heavy footsteps pounded the floor as someone headed our way.

"Is someone in there?" a deep voice asked. "Are you stuck in the elevator?"

It was Mr Murphy! The caretaker! He was still down there. If we didn't do something fast, he'd catch us and give us detention. We might even be suspended or expelled.

"I'm opening the door," Mr Murphy said. "Hold tight!"

Jimmy pushed the GROUND FLOOR button and the elevator went back up.

Above us, I could hear loads of footsteps as people rushed back in. Down below, Mr Murphy was moaning about boxes, a vending machine and chocolates.

When we reached the ground floor, Jimmy pressed his ear against the elevator doors. He raised his hand so I stayed still and quiet. I held my breath, hoping no teachers found us.

The footsteps sounded further away. Soon all I could hear was Jimmy breathing. I was still too scared to breathe myself.

When it was quiet, Jimmy pushed the GROUND FLOOR button again. The doors flew open and he peeked out.

"Let's go," he said. "Run or we'll be late!"

We ran down the narrow corridor, out the basement door and straight upstairs. Everything was a blur until we reached our classroom, getting there just before Mrs Cherry closed the door.

Back at our desks, Jimmy rested his head on his exercise book. I'd never seen him look so tired. My throat was sore from breathing so hard. My legs felt like they needed a good lie down.

"We'll go back tomorrow," Jimmy whispered. "No big deal."

"After we almost got caught? No way!"

"Then you won't solve the case," he said. "If Shelly's guilty, she'll get away with stealing burgers. One day there'll be none left."

He was right, as usual.

"We need more time," I said. "It was silly to think we could catch Shelly and handcuff her in only fifteen minutes. We need more time!"

"How about lunchbreak on Friday?" he said. "We'd have thirty minutes instead of fifteen."

"That's enough time," I said. "Friday lunchtime it is."

"We'll distract the teachers again, but it'll cost you two quid."

"Why so much?"

"Pretending to fight is risky, you know? My friends could've been in serious trouble. We'll have to pay them next time or they won't do it."

"I'm out of pocket money," I said. "You got my last pound the other day."

"I forgot about that."

"Anyway, no more play fights," I said. "The teachers might be suspicious if there's two fights in two days."

"You got a better idea?" he asked. "How should we distract the teachers?"

"By doing something nice," I said.

"What do you mean?"

"The fake fight was something BAD. When we do something bad, teachers stop us."

"That's true," he said.

"Reading your geography poem was something GOOD. When we do something good, teachers *don't* stop us."

"You're right," he said. "Mrs Cherry let me finish my good poem. That gave you time to get the key. She didn't let them finish their bad fight. That's why we ran out of time."

"We need another good distraction to

keep the teachers busy," I said. "They won't stop the distraction if they're busy enjoying it."

What would be a GOOD distraction? I thought, looking around the classroom for clues.

Maybe some artwork?

No, that wouldn't work. It would only take a few seconds to look at paintings and drawings. We needed something to keep each teacher busy for thirty minutes.

What about another poem?

No, that wouldn't work either. It would have to be a VERY long poem to last for thirty minutes.

What about music?

My eyes drifted to the music cupboard. It was full of instruments to play, but we weren't allowed to take them outside

Then I remembered what Mrs Cherry said

in our first ever music class.

"It takes days to learn the xylophone, months to learn the guitar, and years to learn the piano. Learning to play an instrument is hard, but anything worth doing is hard."

"But Miss, I can't play anything well," Angel cried. "Music is too hard!"

"When things are hard, we're tempted to give up and walk away," Mrs Cherry said. "Don't ever give up. Believe in yourself. Keep trying!"

"Other people have played the recorder before," Jimmy said. "I don't know how to play anything. Not even the triangle…"

"That's not true," Mrs Cherry said. "We were all born with the greatest instrument there ever was. We've played it since the day we were born."

"What instrument is that?" I asked.

"I'll give you some clues," she said. "The

instrument is unique to each of us. Some people have a low one and some have a high one. Some have a quiet one and some have a loud one. Some play this instrument all the time while others barely play it at all."

"What instrument is that?" I asked.

"Your voice," she said. "And my voice. And Angel's, Jimmy's, Emma's…"

That music lesson, we sang so many songs together. We all sang really badly, but we had so much fun that nobody cared.

Singing together again would be a great distraction in the playground, I thought. It would keep the teachers busy while Jimmy and I sneaked into the basement.

"Jimmy, I've got an idea," I said. "Tomorrow, let's do something that brings us all together in a good way. It'll be a distraction every teacher will enjoy."

"All of us together?"

"Our whole class," I said. "And then the whole school."

"Our whole class won't help us, will they? What about Angel and her friends? If they help us, it won't be for free. They'll want something in return."

"I know, but we need everyone's help," I said. "A *small* distraction isn't enough for thirty minutes. With thirty students, we'll have a BIG distraction to keep the teachers busy!"

"Let's talk to everyone at morning breaktime," he said. "We'll ask them for help. We'll offer them something in return. If they say no, we'll think of something else."

"They'll definitely say yes!"

"How do you know?"

"Because we'll copy what my dad does at work."

"What does he do?"

"If he wants to work with someone, he gives them three choices: a good offer, a great offer and the best offer."

"What happens after that?"

"He asks them to choose *one* of the offers," I said. "If he only gave them one offer, they might say no. But when there's three offers, they're too busy picking one to say no."

"Hopefully it'll work for us too," he said. "We'll make *three* offers. Our class will accept an offer and help us in return."

"Exactly!"

"But what could we offer them?" He pulled out his pockets. "I'm out of money. I just bought a new video game yesterday!"

"We won't offer any money," I said. "We'll offer three things every kid in school would love to have..."

Chapter 22

It was Friday. If I didn't catch Shelly today, I might never get another chance. She could run away on the weekend and we'd never see her again. She'd keep stealing burgers from schools until there were none left.

But I wouldn't let that happen.

The morning breaktime bell rang. When we reached the playground, Jimmy and I gathered our class by the big tree.

"Hurry up," Angel snapped. "I've got things to do."

"This won't take long," I said. "Jimmy

and I need everyone's help. It's about the missing burgers. We know who's taking them."

"Is it Mr Badal?" Liam asked. "He's always doing mean things."

"Is it you, Angel?" Emma asked. "You can be really MEAN sometimes."

"Or maybe it's Mya," Angel said. "She's always sneaking around doing top secret things."

Angel was trying to make me angry. She thought I would argue with her. Well, she was wrong. We only had fifteen minutes' break. I wouldn't waste time fighting with her.

"The burger thief's name will be kept secret until she's in detention," I said. "Anyway, does it really matter who the thief is?"

Some people shook their heads. Others

shrugged. Angel rolled her eyes at me.

"To stop the burger thief, Jimmy and I must sneak into a secret room at school. We can't say where we're going. It's too dangerous and we don't want anyone following us."

Our class started whispering to each other. I could hear all the gossip. People thought we were sneaking into the Year Six classroom, Mr Badal's office or the nursery. Big kids weren't allowed in the nursery play area without permission.

No one guessed we were going into the basement...

"While we're sneaking away, you'll have to distract the teachers by singing to them," I said. "Could you guys do that for us?"

"I'm not helping you lot," Angel said. "If you get into trouble, we'll ALL be in trouble. You got me in serious trouble when you stayed at my house!"

"What happened?" Emma asked.

"Because of Mya, my parents sold our five-bedroom house for a three-bedroom one. They gave away half my toys to kids who don't have lots of money. Worst of all, we might only go on TWO holidays this year!"

"That sounds okay to me," Emma said. "I've never been on holiday…"

"Angel's fibbing," I said. "Her parents selling their house is NOT my fault!"

"Yes, it is!" Angel spat.

"No, it's not!" I spat back.

"Yes, it totally is!"

"No, it's…"

I stopped myself.

If she wanted to spend all breaktime arguing, she could do it with someone else. I was too busy to fight with her. I had a case to solve.

"None of you will be in trouble," I said. "Jimmy and I won't tell anyone you helped us. It'll be a secret."

"So, who's gonna help us?" Jimmy asked. "Just put your hand up, okay?"

I looked around, hoping to see at least half the class raise their hand. Instead, out of twenty-eight people, ONE person put their hand up.

"I'll help," Libby said quietly. Her voice trembled because she's really shy.

Libby was the quietest, nicest person in the whole school. I knew I could count on her, but we needed more than one person.

Time for Plan B, I thought. Copy what Dad does at work.

When Dad wanted someone to accept his offer, he gave them three different choices. The first choice was good. The second choice was great. The third choice was AMAZING.

So, all I had to do was give our class three different offers: a good one, a great one and an amazing one. In return, they'd keep the teachers busy while Jimmy and I sneaked into the basement.

"Lucky you, Libby," I said happily. "You get one of three gifts. It's a shame no one else in class gets one. Oh well…"

Jimmy and I walked away. A moment later, our class called us back.

"What're the gifts, Mya?" Emma asked. "I might want one too!"

"You probably won't," I said. "Forget I said anything, okay?"

"Please tell us," Liam cried.

"I want to know too!" Patrice said.

"I'll help you guys if I get a gift," Eve said. "Can we have more than one gift? Maybe two…or all three?"

When Angel heard that, her eyes narrowed

and she smiled. It was her mean smile that meant she was up to no good…

"Only ONE gift," Jimmy said. "Mya, tell them the first gift they can choose."

It was time to share what the GOOD gift was.

"Your first choice is one chocolate bar each," I said. "You'll get it at lunchtime over the next few weeks."

"Why not straight away?" Angel asked. "I want mine now!"

"If we hand out twenty-eight chocolate bars right away, the whole school will notice. Then they'll want one too. If they don't get one, they'll moan to Mrs Cherry. She'll start asking questions and find out everything!"

That was all a giant fib.

The real reason they wouldn't get their chocolate straight away was because I didn't have enough money. It would cost twenty-eight pounds. My piggy bank was empty!

"Can we have any chocolate or sweet we want?" Emma asked.

"Nothing that costs more than a pound," Jimmy said. "Before you decide which chocolate or sweet you want, Mya will tell us about the second gift. Remember, you can only choose *one*."

It was time to share what the GREAT gift was. I crossed my fingers and hoped they would like it.

"The second gift is…tutoring!"

"Boring!" Angel snapped. "We learn enough at school every day."

"Not everyone gets the top grades like you and Mya," Jimmy said. "The rest of us wannabe really smart too."

"Can you make us really smart?" Emma asked.

"I can try," I said. "Getting the top grades

in class is really cool. We get special things others don't!"

"Like what?" Emma asked.

"You know our class gets a treat at the end of the year. Usually it's a box of chocolates we've got to share." I lowered my voice. "Everyone with the top grades gets a top secret reward! We don't have to share it with anyone."

"I've never got one of those," Angel said. "No fair…"

There wasn't really a secret reward for really, really smart kids. Everyone in class got treated the same.

"My parents reward me, too," I said. "When I get top marks, I get a present. I can have whatever I want. It's like Christmas and my birthday came early!"

"What about your homework?" Jimmy asked. "Because you're so smart, you finish your work really quickly, right?"

"Yep. Then I can get back to fun stuff like playing with toys or watching TV."

"My homework takes SO long," Emma said. "I want to finish quickly too so I can play with my new dolls."

"Me too," Eve cried. "I definitely want the tutoring gift, not chocolate."

"Wait a second," Jimmy said. "Mya has one more gift to offer. Then you can choose the one you want."

It was time to tell them about the AMAZING gift. I couldn't think of any better gift to give.

"The last gift is called...Prefect Power!"

The whole class stopped talking. Some people looked amazed while others looked confused.

"I know the Head Prefect," I said. "He's my friend. He uses his Prefect badge to help me. It's got me out of trouble a few times."

"Could he help us too?" Emma asked.

"Only if you help Jimmy and me," I said. "If you ever need help, just call me and Prefect Power will save you."

"How?" Angel asked.

"If you're caught being naughty, the Head Prefect will stick up for you. Teachers won't tell you off when he's around."

"Liar!" Angel spat. "Anyway, what if Mr Badal tells us off? I bet Prefect Power doesn't work then!"

People were nodding and agreeing with her. They thought Prefect Power wouldn't work against Mr Badal. I had to prove them wrong.

"Did you hear about the girl who was sick on Mr Badal's new carpet?" I asked. "That was me."

"No way!" someone cried.

"I can't believe it!" Emma said. "Did you get detention?"

"Nope," I said. "Do you know why?"

"Prefect Power!" everyone cried.

"Exactly," I said. "I could've been sick on Mr Badal's brand-new shoes and nothing would've happened because of Prefect Power! When the Head Prefect is your friend, not even the headteacher can stop you!"

Their mouths were hanging open. Even Angel looked surprised, and then angry. She crossed her arms and turned away. I didn't mind though, because I didn't care.

"My mum always says we should read the small print," Angel said, her back still facing me.

"What's a "small print"?" Emma asked.

"The small print is something they're keeping secret about the offer," Angel said. "Something they don't want us to know…"

Everyone turned to me. I gulped.

"Okay, there IS a small print," I said. "The Head Prefect is very busy with Year Six work. You know how tough it is. He can't help us all the time, so you only get Prefect Power THREE times and then that's it."

"I knew Prefect Power sounded too good to be true," Angel said. "I will NOT be choosing that gift…"

"There's more small print too," I said. "Prefect Power can't be used by anyone who's been REALLY bad. That means no bullying, stealing, rude words, hitting, kicking or breaking stuff on purpose. If you do any of that, you're on your own."

"Sounds fair to me," Emma said. "Bullies don't deserve Prefect Power!"

Jimmy raised his hand so everyone was quiet. When the class was silent, he finally spoke.

"Everyone, Mya has given you three gifts to choose from: one chocolate or sweet, tutoring and homework help, or...PREFECT POWER!"

People started whispering to each other. I couldn't tell what they would choose. I just hoped that we had enough help to keep the teachers busy.

"Time's up," I said. "Mrs Cherry will be out soon."

"Hands up if you want a chocolate bar or sweet," Jimmy said. He counted the raised hands. "That's two...three...four of you."

"That'll only be four pounds," I whispered. "I can borrow that from Will!"

"Okay, everyone. Hands up if you want tutoring and homework help." Jimmy counted each hand. "Seven of you want to be smarter. Cool!"

Angel looked back and stuck her tongue

out at me. I just turned my head the other way. Out the corner of my eye, I could see her face turning red.

"And the last gift was...the wonderful, amazing, brilliant Prefect Power!"

Many hands shot up before Jimmy could finish speaking. He counted them quickly and then recounted just in case.

"How many?" I asked.

"Sixteen people want Prefect Power!" Jimmy said. "I'd choose that one too!"

That was it, I thought. Our class had agreed to help us. At lunchbreak, they would sing songs to keep the teachers busy. It would give Jimmy and me enough time to catch the burger thief!

"Mya, you'll have a VERY busy weekend," Jimmy whispered. "There's lots to do!"

He was right.

I had to buy four chocolates, start tutoring

seven people, and ask Jamar the Head Prefect to help sixteen people stay out of trouble.

Four chocolates.

Seven students to tutor.

Sixteen people with Prefect Power.

Four. Seven. Sixteen.

Four plus seven plus sixteen equals twenty-seven. Twenty-seven people had picked a gift.

But there were twenty-eight people in class, not including Jimmy and me.

Someone hadn't voted.

"Wait a second," I said. "Someone hasn't voted yet. Are you still thinking about it?"

No one answered.

"Who didn't vote?" I asked.

"Mrs Cherry is coming out now," Jimmy said. "We'll vote again! Quickly!"

Jimmy asked who wanted a chocolate bar or sweet. Four hands went up.

Next, he asked who wanted tutoring and homework help. Seven hands went up.

Last, he asked who wanted PREFECT POWER. Sixteen hands went up.

While people were voting, I kept looking around to see whose hand never went up.

Can you guess who it was?

"Angel…"

"Yes, Mya?" She turned to face me, grinning from ear to ear. "Can I help you?"

"Yes," I said through gritted teeth. "You could put your hand up!"

"I want to vote, but I'd like a fourth choice, please."

"A fourth one? What is it?"

"You won't like it…"

"Just say it," I said. "What gift would you like?"

Angel rushed over to me. She leaned in and lowered her voice so only Jimmy and I could hear.

"Can I have any gift I want?" she asked.

"Depends what it is," I said.

"Okay, I want my gift to be a whole month in detention."

"Why do you want detention?" I asked.

"*I* won't be in detention," she said. "YOU will be in detention!"

"But I haven't done anything wrong!"

"Not yet," she said. "Not until you go into the basement."

Uh oh…Angel had figured out our plan.

"You're wrong," I said. "We're not going into the basement."

"You are! I *know* you are!"

"You're lying," I said. "If you're gonna tell fibs about us, no gift for you!"

"But you promised everybody a gift," she said. "We can pick any gift we want!"

"Choose something, then!"

"My gift is you getting detention!"

"No," I hissed. "I won't give you a horrible gift like that. Choose something else!"

"Fine then," she said. "If you won't give me the detention gift, I'm sure Mrs Cherry will. She'll give you a whole month in detention when she finds out what you're up to!"

Angel dashed across the playground. Jimmy and I ran after her, begging her to keep our secret. She laughed and ran even faster until she reached Mrs Cherry.

Jimmy and I stopped close by.

"I'll take the blame," I said. "Go back to the others, okay?"

"When I was stuck in Mr Murphy's room, you could've left me behind, but you didn't." Jimmy took my hand and squeezed it before letting go. "I'm not leaving you. Friends don't do that."

Together, we walked over to Mrs Cherry and Angel. Angel didn't say anything until Jimmy and I got there.

"Mya and Jimmy just told us a secret," Angel said. "Miss, can you guess what the secret is?"

"No, Angel," Mrs Cherry said. "I bet you'll tell me."

Angel spun to face me. "Should I tell her or do you want to?"

"I…I…Please don't."

"Okay, fine! I'll tell her," Angel said. "Mrs Cherry, Jimmy and Mya are working on something top secret. I think it has something to do with the basement…"

Chapter 23

"The basement?" Mrs Cherry cried. "But no one's allowed down there!"

"No, Miss, not the *school* basement," Angel said. "I'm talking about the basement at my house. Jimmy and Mya have something top secret planned down there."

Angel turned to me, her narrow, blue eyes glaring. Usually I'd glare back, but I didn't want to make her even madder.

"I think they're planning a sleepover party in my basement," she said. "The last time we had one, Mya burst my waterbed. She never even said sorry."

"Sorry," I mumbled.

"Oh, guess what else happened, Miss?" Angel asked.

"What, dear?"

"Jimmy said I was the prettiest girl in the whole school, didn't you?"

"Yeah, whatever."

"I beg your pardon?" Angel's eyes slit. "Say that again?"

"You're the prettiest girl in the whole school," he grumbled.

"That's very nice, dear," Mrs Cherry said. "A sleepover sounds like so much fun! For a moment there, I thought you were talking about the school basement…"

"Nope, I meant *my* basement," Angel said. "We're not allowed in the school basement."

"Definitely not," Mrs Cherry said. "Stay away from it! It's dreadful, terrible,

HORRIBLE down there. There are spiders, rats, mice and…and very scary ghosts!"

"Scary ghosts?" Angel asked. "Are there really ghosts down there?"

"I have to go," Mrs Cherry said, rushing off. "Stay away from the basement and behave yourselves!"

Mrs Cherry went to the other teachers. They talked quietly, stopping whenever students got too close.

"Teachers can be so weird," Angel said. "Anyway, you two should thank me!"

"For what?" I asked.

"For not telling the truth. I still can, you know?" She stuck her tongue out at me. "Anyway, you'd better be nice to me for the next month or I'll tell MR BADAL everything, okay?"

Jimmy and I nodded.

"I can't HEAR you!"

"Yes, Angel," we both said.

"By the way, I wasn't lying when I said I wanted the fourth choice. I don't want chocolate or tutoring or Prefect Power...I want chocolate AND tutoring AND Prefect Power!"

"But Mya said you can only pick one!" Jimmy cried. "Everyone else gets one. Why should you get three gifts?"

"Angel, you can have them all," I said quickly. "Just leave us alone, okay?"

"See you soon," she said. "I hope you get caught in the basement by the spiders, rats, mice and ghosts!"

She skipped off to her friends. They pointed at us and laughed.

"Why'd you give her all three gifts?" Jimmy asked.

"If she tells on us, we'll be stuck in detention for weeks! And we'll lose our badges! We can't be police officers without them."

Jimmy nodded, frowning at Angel and her mean friends.

"You're right," he said. "Besides, we only have to be nice to her for one month. After that, we can be mean again!"

We laughed. Angel and her friends didn't like that. They stuck out their tongues at us and walked off in a huff.

Mrs Cherry blew her whistle. Breaktime was over. Next playtime was lunchbreak. That's when we'd go into the basement.

Our class came over to line up. Everyone gave a thumbs up. That made me smile. It was nice knowing we had so much help, even though some help came from mean people like Angel.

"Mya," Jimmy whispered, "soon we'll be in the basement! I can't wait to tell my friends in Year Five. They won't believe me!"

"We should bring something back from the basement," I said. "Something to prove we were down there."

"Great idea! There must be some cool stuff hidden down there. Maybe things from a hundred years ago!"

"We'll find out soon," I said. "Just a few hours to go…"

Chapter 24

The hours dragged on and on and on. That always happens when you're looking forward to something.

When the lunch bell rang, the whole class fell silent. Mrs Cherry sat at her desk, looking very confused. She watched us quietly line up at the door.

"Is there something I should know about?" she asked.

"No, Miss," I said. "We're just behaving ourselves. It's the right thing to do."

On the way downstairs, we kept quiet and

stuck together. We couldn't talk about the basement plan around other classes. They might tell on us.

In the lunch hall, our class sat together so we could plan our musical performance. Lunchtime was our last chance to get everything right before playtime.

Every time the dinner ladies walked past our tables, we stopped talking. We didn't want them to hear our plan.

"Is everything all right?" a dinner lady asked. "Anything you kids want to share?"

"The food was tasty," Jimmy said. "I wish I could have more."

"Oh, thank you..."

The dinner lady left the hall and came back with Mrs Cherry. They both looked nervous while they watched our class.

The bell rang.

It was time to go outside. Quietly, we

walked out with our heads held high. Everyone watched us, wondering what was going on.

When we got outside, I looked around the playground. I couldn't see Shelly. She had to be inside somewhere. Maybe in the toilets. Maybe in her classroom. Maybe in the basement...

Our class stopped in the middle of the playground, so everyone could see us. I stayed at the back with Jimmy. As we agreed, Angel got to be at the front with her friends. I didn't like Angel getting her own way, but we had to do it or she'd tell on us.

"Is everyone ready?" Angel asked.

We all nodded.

The teachers gathered near the doors, whispering to each other. Mrs Cherry had her whistle ready to blow. Mr Badal came out, ready to shout. The other kids were nearby, watching our class.

Angel stepped forward so all eyes were on her. She said, "Ladies and gentlemen, boys and girls, teachers and students, rich and poor—"

"Get on with it," I hissed.

"I am!" Angel spat. She was loving the attention. "I'm going to…I mean *we* are going to sing a brand-new song. We wrote it about our amazing school. The song is called Angel and Friends."

I wanted to call the song Let's Have Fun, but Angel had to get her own way…

Our class held hands, swaying together like a music group. Then we cleared our throats and raised our hands to the sky. It felt like we were touching the clouds.

"We're an amazing school with amazing kids," Angel sang. "That isn't a lie, that isn't a fib."

We nodded together, smiling.

"We're sorry for yesterday's big fight. Today we're gonna do what's right."

We went to the other kids and pulled them into our singing group. Jimmy and I stayed at the back, so we could sneak off without being seen.

"Join in while we sing our song," Angel sang off-key. "If we all sing together, we can't go wrong."

All the teachers and students sang together. It didn't matter what song it was. We sang everything from nursery rhymes to pop tunes. People were laughing and joking and dancing. It was the best playtime ever!

It was a shame I couldn't stay!

Jimmy and I danced together, moving closer and closer to the doors. When the teachers all had their backs turned, we sneaked inside.

We stopped by the basement door.

"Are you ready?" I asked.

"Yep," he said. "Let's do this!"

When I opened the basement door, the narrow corridor looked different. Last time, it was so bright and white. This time, it was shadowy and dark.

"It's so creepy in here," I whispered. "Where's the light switch?"

"Maybe it's by the elevator."

We tiptoed through the darkness, our eyes on the bright elevator ahead.

Suddenly the basement door slammed shut behind us, plunging the corridor into more darkness. It got even darker when the elevator doors closed. Was someone in there?

"Did you see anyone?" I asked.

"Yeah…"

"Well? Who was it?"

"Shelly."

That's why she hadn't been outside. She must've hidden until lunchtime was over. Then she could sneak into the basement without being spotted.

But how did she get a basement key? We had Mrs Cherry's basement key, so Shelly must've taken Mr Murphy or Mr Badal's.

If Shelly was getting help from dinner ladies, the nurse, the caretaker and the headteacher, this case was much bigger than we'd thought. I couldn't arrest all those people, could I? I'd never arrested an adult before. I wasn't sure if it was even allowed.

But we couldn't turn back now. It was Friday. She might be destroying evidence by eating it. Come Monday, all proof she was the burger thief would be gone. My secret boss would be really, *really* angry with me!

"Jimmy, keep going straight ahead," I said, struggling to see him in the dark. "We'll get to the elevator soon."

Slowly we walked through the darkness until we reached the light switch. I turned on the lights.

"Handcuffs ready?" I asked.

"Check!"

"Badge ready?"

"Check!"

"Ready to go?"

"Yep!"

My hand was shaking when I pressed the elevator button.

"Are you sure about this?" I asked. "It's not too late to go back."

"No going back this time," he said. "I'm not leaving without her."

"…Me neither!"

When the elevator doors opened, Jimmy and I stepped inside. I pushed the BASEMENT button.

Slowly we went down.

And down.

And down…

The elevator stopped.

The doors flew open but neither of us moved. When we saw the school basement, we couldn't believe our eyes…

Chapter 25

THIS was the basement? Where were the spiderwebs and creepy crawlies? Where was the giant rat nibbling on smelly cheese? Where was the scary ghost? Where was the smell of damp? Where was the dripping sound from a leaky pipe? And where were the shadows and darkness?

I couldn't see any of that because the school basement was…AMAZING!!!!!

There were no windows, but it was so bright down there. And it was HUGE. There was a mini basketball court with cute little hoops. Close by was a vending machine full of fizzy drinks, chocolate and sweets. They all looked so tasty!

I went over to a comfy-looking sofa and sat down. It was a great place to watch the widescreen television with huge speakers! Underneath the TV were lots of movies, a DVD player, a games console and the latest video games.

"Mya, look at this!" Jimmy cried. "A gym!"

I ran over to the gym area. It had lots of exercise machines including a treadmill, bike and even a bench for lifting heavy weights. Jimmy jumped on the exercise bike and started pedalling really fast.

Should I exercise too? Or should I get some chocolate and chill out on the sofa?

I didn't know what to do first!

No wonder the teachers kept this place a

secret. If other students knew about the basement, they'd never leave. I didn't want to go myself. Everywhere I looked there was more to do. I could've stayed down there forever.

Suddenly Jimmy stopped cycling.

"Did you hear that?" he asked. "I heard someone sniffing."

I hadn't heard anything but him puffing away. He was so fit, just like my dad.

My dad worked out six days a week. He went for a five-minute walk around the block. He said it was good for the body. Mum said he was lazy and should do more, but he said no.

"Mya, just listen…There it is again!"

Jimmy got off the bike and tiptoed across the room. He stopped by the vending machine and pressed his ear against it. Then he waved me over.

"Someone's on the other side," he whispered in my ear. "Shelly, maybe?"

"I'm going in," I said. "If I'm not back in one minute, get help. Call my dad. Tell him not to be angry. Don't call Mum or I'll be in bigger trouble!"

"No way," Jimmy said. "We're doing this together. We're a team, remember?" He patted me on the back. "Ladies first."

Oh great...

I edged closer to the sniffing person, armed with my badge and handcuffs.

Feeling a bit nervous, I wished I knew karate like my brother. Will said he could fight fifty people at the same time. He said he could do it with his eyes closed and his feet tied together. I didn't believe him. Fifty people sounds like a lot. Thirty people maybe, but not fifty.

"This is Detective Inspector Mya Dove

and Detective Inspector Jimmy..."

"Jimmy'll do," he whispered.

"Yes. Jimmy. We have badges to show we are REAL police officers, not fake ones like on TV." I slid my badge across the floor. A chubby, white hand reached out and snatched it. "See? It's real."

I stepped closer and closer, trying not to tremble. Police officers shouldn't show they're afraid. We're supposed to stay brave and strong. Good thing Jimmy was right behind me, holding my hand.

"Come out with your hands up," I said. "You have one more chance."

Nothing. Not a word.

"Okay, okay, I'll give you *one* more chance to turn yourself in."

The suspect tossed my badge back, but they didn't come out. That made me VERY ANGRY. It was rude to toss my poor, little badge like that!

"Now you've made me mad! Jimmy, I'm going in!" I let go of his hand and rushed round the vending machine. "Put your hands...up?"

There she was. Shelly. Curled up in a ball. Crying. Her eyes were pink and puffy. There was a huge snot bubble in her nose and more snot trickled down her lips.

"Shelly Walters," I said, showing my badge, "you're under arrest for stealing ten burgers from the school kitchen. Anything you say will be written down and given to Mr Badal. If found guilty, you'll be in detention for at least two weeks. Shelly, are you guilty or not guilty?"

"Guilty."

Well, that was unexpected. I thought she'd blame someone else. Nope. She stood up and put the handcuffs on herself. Still crying, she headed for the elevator.

"Cool, let's go," Jimmy said, following her. "I can't wait to get back outside. Terry said I can't sing. I'm gonna show him who's the best singer at school!"

That was it? It was over already? No way. It was too easy. Why didn't she lie? Or try to run away? It was like she wanted me to arrest her, but why?

"Shelly, wait a minute!" I ran past her and blocked the elevator. "I have some questions first."

"Why?" she asked. "You got what you wanted."

"What do you mean by that?"

She sighed. "You wanted to set me up. You think I'm the burger thief just because I'm fat."

"It's not because you're fat," I fibbed. "It's because you're...blonde? No, I mean it's because you're…short? No, I mean…"

I shut my mouth and kept quiet.

"Look, I've tried to be skinny but nothing's worked," she said. "Maybe going to detention will help. At least I'll be away from all the food..."

Is that why she said she was guilty? So we'd keep her away from food?

"Yes," she said, like she was reading my mind. "Not eating is hard. My stomach hurts. It just keeps grumbling all day. I gave it water but it still won't shut up."

Shelly grabbed her tummy and squeezed really hard. It looked painful.

"What about the food in the vending machine?" I asked. "Don't you eat that?"

"I don't have enough pocket money," she said. "Anyway, I'm glad I can't buy anything in there. I'd probably eat it all if I could because my belly just won't stop…"

Her stomach grumbled loudly. She smacked it.

"Stop it," I snapped. "Be nice to your belly. It's the only one you've got."

She looked surprised, and then she smiled a bit.

"Thanks...Not used to people being nice to me."

She walked over to the basketball court and grabbed the ball. Still wearing the handcuffs, she took a shot. The ball flew through the hoop easily. Then she turned to the other hoop and took another shot. The ball spun around the hoop before falling through the net.

"You play?" Jimmy asked. "Why don't you ever play with us?"

"You never asked," she said. "I want to be a basketball star someday but..."

"But what?" Jimmy stood beside her.

"You're really good!"

"Yeah, but I'm too fat. No one ever wants to play with me. In P.E., people don't pick the fat kid until we're the only one left."

I remembered Nurse Mona saying Shelly played basketball, but I hadn't believed her. Fat people don't play sports, right?

But Shelly was fat and played a sport. She was good at it, too. We just never realised because nobody gave her a chance to play. We all thought she was too fat and too lazy. That's why she was always picked last in P.E. class.

"I'm so sorry," I said. "I should've given you a proper chance."

"It's okay. I'm used to it." She shrugged.

"No. It's NOT okay." I took her hand and squeezed it. "We were mean to you. I feel like a bully!"

"Whoa, you're not a bully," Shelly said

quickly. "Angel is a bully. You just didn't give me a chance, that's all. Most kids don't. Even some adults don't. That's why I want to lose weight. Then everyone will be nicer to me. If I'm skinny, people will like me."

"No, Shelly," I said. "You shouldn't have to be skinny for us to be nice to you. We should be nice to you anyway, skinny or not. That's just the right thing to do."

Shelly gave me a hug. I squeezed her back. She was so soft and cuddly. I didn't want to let go, but we had to leave before we got caught.

We rode the elevator upstairs and locked the basement door. Shelly showed us her key. She'd borrowed it from Mr Murphy. All the teachers knew she was down there, but they didn't mind.

"In the basement, I can hide from all the tasty food." Her stomach grumbled. "I haven't lost any weight yet, but it'll happen soon."

"Are you sure?" I asked. "Your stomach sounds really upset. Maybe it'd be best to eat something."

Shelly and Jimmy looked really, really confused.

"I want to lose weight, but you're telling me to...eat?"

"That's what my mum does to keep fit," I said. "She eats more vegetables and fruit instead of burgers and pizza. I've never seen her stop eating ALL food."

"And that keeps her fit?" Shelly asked.

"Very fit! Yesterday she worked out for thirty whole minutes!"

"She must be really tired afterwards," Shelly said. "I'm always tired after basketball."

"Mum's got lots of energy left," I said.

"After working out, she takes a quick shower and goes to work at the hospital."

"Wow! I want to have lots of energy!" Shelly cried. "Does being fit make her prettier, too? I want to be pretty like other girls."

"You're already pretty," Jimmy said. "You both are."

My cheeks felt so warm when he said that…

"Healthy food makes my mum very pretty," I said. "Veg and fruit keep her afro hair nice and long. If you stretch it, it reaches her bum. I hope mine gets that long soon."

"So, I shouldn't stop eating?"

"Nah! Try different food like veg. You can still have burgers, just not ten."

"…What're you talking about?" she asked.

"The ten missing school burgers."

Shelly glared at me. I knew I'd said

something wrong.

"I didn't steal ANY burgers!"

"Sorry," I said. "You said you were guilty, so I thought—"

"I did steal some salad twice, but I NEVER stole burgers!"

"I thought—"

"Does everyone think I stole the missing burgers? Just because I'm fat?" She wiped tears from her eyes. "Mr Badal won't buy burgers anymore. Why does everyone blame ME?"

She burst into tears again, so I gave her another hug.

"Well, everyone is wrong," I said. "You didn't steal the burgers. It's easier to blame you instead of Mr Badal because he's really mean and scary."

"Will you tell everyone that for me?" she asked.

"Tell them what? That Mr Badal's mean and scary?"

"No, they know that already," she said. "I mean tell everyone that I didn't steal the burgers. You believe me, right?"

"Yes, I do."

"Could you make the other kids believe me, too?"

"I'll try, but I can't MAKE them do anything they don't want to."

"You can try right now," Jimmy said. "It's gone quiet out there. We missed the playground party…"

"Thanks, Mya!" Shelly hugged me. "I know I can count on you!"

They wanted me to tell the whole school that Shelly wasn't the burger thief, but…I didn't know what to say! And I was REALLY scared!

I was great at giving speeches to my class,

but only thirty people were there. I knew them all because we'd grown up together.

This speech would be different. The school had nine hundred people in it. Most of them I'd never met before.

My legs trembled. My throat tightened. It was hard to breathe and got even harder as we walked outside.

No going back now.

Jimmy whistled, getting everyone's attention. They all looked really tired from all that dancing and singing.

"Mya has something very important to say," Jimmy cried. "Go on, Mya…"

I didn't know what to say. My mind was as blank as plain paper. The whole school staring at me didn't help. It just made me more nervous.

Then I remembered what Jimmy said days ago: "It's okay to be scared. Being scared means you're about to do something really, really brave."

It was time to be brave.

After a very deep breath, I was finally ready to speak. I didn't have anything planned. I wasn't even sure what to say. So, I just focused on helping Shelly.

"Hello, everyone," I said, a big lump in my throat. "I've got something important to say."

That's how I started a speech our school would never forget. After that day, things would never be the same...

Chapter 26

It was time to give my speech to the whole playground. Shelly wanted me to stick up for her. Jimmy made sure I had everyone's attention. Angel was giving me dirty looks, as usual. Probably because everyone was looking at me instead of her.

"Go on, Mya," Jimmy whispered. "I'm right here."

"Me too," Shelly whispered. "I've been feeling so lonely. It's nice knowing I have a friend at school."

Friends don't let friends down.

Police officers don't let people down either. Doing hard things was part of my job. After such a tough week, I couldn't give up now. Not when Shelly needed my help.

If I was nicer to Shelly, maybe everyone else would be nicer too? I did the same thing with my friend Libby. People thought she was mean because she kept quiet. When they gave her a chance, they realised quiet people are just like everyone else, but quieter. Shelly was just like everyone else too, but fatter.

"What's wrong, Mya?" Mrs Cherry asked. "Go on, dear. We're listening."

I stepped forward.

"I just wanted to say...Shelly Walters is NOT the burger thief!"

The other kids gasped. The adults all looked confused.

"Shelly is not guilty. She didn't steal the burgers. Nobody did."

"Liar," Angel snapped. "There were ten fewer burgers than usual. Everyone knows it." She pointed at Shelly. "See how fat she is? Because she eats all the food!"

"Actually, she isn't eating at all."

Everyone stared at Shelly. Her teary eyes fell to the ground.

"But everyone *has* to eat," Angel said. "If you don't eat, you'll be sick."

Angel looked sorry for Shelly. I couldn't believe it! Angel feeling sorry for anyone but herself never happened. I rubbed my eyes and looked again, just in case I was imagining things. I wasn't.

"Why did she stop eating?" Angel asked.

"Well, ask her!" I took Shelly by the hand and pulled her forward. "Talk to her. She's like the rest of us, just fatter. She plays games like us too. You should see her play basketball."

Jimmy stepped forward and said, "From now on, I want Shelly on my basketball team. We've been losing for ages, but not anymore."

The other basketball players looked very surprised.

"Shelly might be the best basketball player in school," Jimmy said, "but we never gave her a chance because she's fat. Being fat doesn't stop her from making shots!"

The teachers looked very proud of us. Mr Badal even smiled a little.

"So," Angel said, "what about the missing burgers? The dinner ladies said they forgot to order them. What really happened? If Shelly didn't eat them, where did the burgers go?"

"Nowhere," I replied. "They were never here."

The other kids gasped.

"My secret source told me the government

doesn't want us eating burgers at school anymore. They think burgers will make us too fat."

"Fat like me..." Shelly wiped a tear from her cheek.

"Being fat isn't healthy," I said, "but at least she's very fit. Being fit is healthy. We bash fat people for being lazy, but how many people here exercise?"

Only a few people put their hand up.

I wasn't one of them.

"Wait a minute," Angel said. "If Shelly exercises, why is she so fat?"

"I don't know why she's fat, but we'll figure it out." I turned to Shelly. "What I do know is that not eating makes people sick. That's why your stomach hurts so much. You're really, really, really hungry, and that's not good."

The teachers were nodding, so I knew I

was on the right track. I just had to keep going.

"Fat people need help so they can lose weight. Bullying them isn't helpful. It makes them do dangerous things like not eating."

"Mya is right," a familiar voice said. "Absolutely right!"

Everyone turned to see who was speaking. I peered through the crowd and saw a familiar, friendly face. If anyone could help with my important speech, it was her...

Chapter 27

Who was coming to help me? Nurse Mona! She squeezed through the crowd and stood beside me. I felt better knowing she was there. She knew all about getting fit and being healthy.

"Mya is right about unhealthy eating habits," Nurse Mona said. "Not eating is dangerous. The body needs food like a car needs petrol. Without the right fuel, the body, and car, go nowhere."

The adults nodded in agreement.

"I lost weight many times in my life,"

Nurse Mona said. "I'm an old woman now, but better late than never. So, why have I stayed fit this time? Because now I am eating for the right reasons."

"What are the right reasons to eat?" Shelly asked. "I eat when I'm very happy, like at Christmas, or very sad, like when my dog died."

"It's best to only eat when you're *hungry*," Nurse Mona said. "When I'm happy, I celebrate without eating. For example, at Christmas we try not to overeat. Instead of eating all day, we play games, watch festive TV shows, and dance to the best Christmas songs ever."

"What about when I'm sad?" Shelly asked. "What can I do instead of eating?"

"When I'm sad or angry, I go for a five-minute walk. You could walk around the playground until you feel better. Walking is more helpful than eating food you don't really want."

Shelly looked much happier for a moment, but then she looked sad again.

"What's wrong?" Nurse Mona asked.

"If I want to be healthier, I've got so much to learn." She threw her hands up. "It's a lot to think about! I can't eat too much food, I can't eat too little food, argh! My head hurts…"

"I know the feeling," Nurse Mona said. "When I started losing weight and getting fit, I had so much to learn that it scared me! It's best to take it one step at a time. One day, one week, one month at a time."

"How do I start?" Shelly asked.

"Make ONE positive change. Build one good habit until it's easier. Then, and only then, will you move on to the next step."

Shelly thought for a moment.

"So just ONE thing?"

Nurse Mona nodded.

"One thing I could do is put more veg on my plate. Or maybe I could drink more water. Basketball always makes me really thirsty!"

"We should ALL do that," Nurse Mona said. "Over time, we could swap a bottle of fizzy drink or juice for some water."

"Water is gross," Angel said. "It doesn't taste of anything!"

"She's right," Shelly said. "Nurse Mona, can we make water taste better?"

"Of course! Add fruit slices to your water jug and let them soak for a few hours. Now your water will taste sweet and fruity!"

I stepped forward to speak again.

"Blending water and fruit makes a great smoothie," I said. "Much better than anything at the shops."

Now the other kids wanted to make smoothies, too. They talked about trying different fruit like apples, pears, bananas and grapes.

Nurse Mona turned to the adults. They gulped, looking nervous. Even Mr Badal looked scared, even though he's in charge of everyone.

"All the adults should make an effort too, not just the kids," Nurse Mona said. "We must set a good example."

Mrs Cherry stepped forward, smiling. She looked very happy about everything being said.

All the other teachers still looked nervous. I guess they hadn't expected Nurse Mona to teach them something, too.

Mrs Cherry asked, "What can we do to help Shelly and the others get fit?"

"Two things to start with," Nurse Mona

said. "First, I suggest giving out health and fitness awards. It will encourage anyone who tries to be healthier and fitter."

"What else do you suggest?" Mrs Cherry asked.

"Really big rewards for the class who tries the hardest to be healthy. I'm sure they'd like new toys for their classroom." Nurse Mona stopped to think and her eyes lit up. "At the end of the year, the healthiest class could go on the most exciting school trip!"

That got everyone talking.

Year Six always got a big trip at the end of the year because it was their last year at primary school. Now our class could get a big school trip too. We just needed to eat more veg, eat less junk food and drink more water.

"Sounds very exciting," Mrs Cherry said, clapping her hands. "We'll have a staff meeting on Monday and discuss your ideas."

Mr Badal and the teachers nodded in agreement.

"One more thing," Nurse Mona said. "If anyone needs help getting fit, being healthy, losing weight, gaining weight or anything else, don't do it alone. That's what family, friends and your doctor are for."

"Do doctors help people lose weight?" Shelly asked.

"Many doctors don't know about losing weight, so they'll send you to a dietician. The dietician will help you eat the right amount of food."

"Okay, I understand now," Shelly said. "When I'm sick, I'll go to the doctor. When I'm unfit, I'll go to the dietician."

"Exactly," Nurse Mona said. "If you keep struggling, you might be sent to a therapist. Therapists talk to you to figure out why you eat too much or too little."

"Couldn't we talk to our parents instead?" Shelly asked.

"You should always tell your parents if you're worried about your health," Nurse Mona said. "If you don't have parents, talk to other adults like grandparents, uncles, aunts, foster carers or even teachers."

"My parents don't know I want to get fit," Shelly said. "Should I tell them?"

"Of course! Ask your parents or guardian if you can join some kids' clubs outside of school. By joining a sports club, you'll learn new skills, get fitter AND make lots of friends."

"I HATE sports," Angel snapped. "What other clubs are there?"

"There are fitness groups and activities for everyone," Nurse Mona said. "It doesn't matter if you love basketball, dancing, cycling, swimming or anything else. Just keep active and keep having fun!"

"When can I start being active?" Shelly asked. "Next week? Next month?"

"Let's start now," Nurse Mona said. "What can we do to start being active? Any ideas, children?"

In the crowd, I saw a fat, white hand go up. When the person came forward, I recognised her straight away. It was Alicia, the fussy Year Six girl. She was with the other fat kids I met days ago. There was Daniel, who was crazy about basketball, Theo, the vegan who saved animals, and Shamima, who stole school ants.

"I'm going to download a free fitness app on my phone," Alicia said. "That'll help me keep active every day!"

"I'll be active by going for walks to the park," Shamima said happily. "I can't wait to see all the bugs there. I won't steal any, I promise…"

"I want to be active and have fun too," Theo cried. "I'll be volunteering at the local farm. It means I can help animals AND get fit at the same time!"

"What about me?" Daniel asked sadly. "I always watch basketball but never play because I'm fat. Do basketball clubs let fat people join?"

"Of course!" Nurse Mona said. "There's a club for everyone. They don't care about your age, race, gender, weight, height or religion. Just go and have fun!"

"Thanks, Nurse Mona," Daniel said. "I'll find a basketball club this weekend. Shelly, we can join one together."

"I'd love that!" she cried.

"Joining a club is a great way to be healthier," Nurse Mona said. "How else can we keep fit?"

I put my hand up to speak.

"My mum is a nurse," I said. "At the hospital, she feeds patients mostly veg. Filling the plate with veggies keeps people full so they don't eat too much."

"Thanks, I'll try that!" Shelly said. "I only stopped eating food because I always ate too much. That won't happen anymore because eating lots of veggies will keep me full."

"We should *all* try that," Mrs Cherry said. "Eating more fruit and vegetables makes you feel better. Not eating anything makes you feel worse."

"Can we pick the school's fruit and veg?" Shelly asked. "I'd love to try sweet potato!"

"That's a great idea," Mrs Cherry said. "Everyone can vote for their favourite fruit and vegetable. The most popular ones will make the menu!"

Mrs Cherry went over to Mr Badal and

they started talking about our lunch. I'd never seen Mr Badal smile so much. I guess he really liked talking about veg and fruit!

All the kids said sorry to Shelly before going inside. I guess they felt guilty about being so mean to her. Even Angel whispered an apology before rushing back to class.

"Mya, thank you," Shelly said. "Now I can eat food and lose weight the healthy way!"

Shelly followed her class back inside.

Jimmy came over with a sad look on his face.

"What's wrong?" I asked.

"I told my friends about the basement, but nobody believes me! They think I'm lying!"

"Good!"

"Good?"

"Going into the basement was part of a top secret investigation," I said. "We shouldn't tell anyone about it."

"You're right," he said. "The Children's Police Force wouldn't be happy that I told my friends about the case."

"They'd take away your badge," I said. "That's why the basement has to be our little secret!"

"Our little secret," he said. "Let's shake on it!"

We shook hands.

On the way back to class, I peeked inside the Year Two classroom. I wanted to see how Shelly was doing. Was she making lots of new friends? Or was she still all alone...?

Chapter 28

When I peeked inside Year Two's classroom, I hoped that Shelly was making friends.

I looked around and spotted her sitting with some boys and girls. They were chatting by the toybox.

"Shelly, where do you live?" a girl asked.

"Opposite Hare Street. Just past the library."

"Me too," the girl cried. "You should come out and play with us!"

Hearing that made me smile. Shelly could make friends instead of being alone. She looked so much happier because people were being nice to her.

"I promise to be nice to everybody, including fat people," I told myself. "It's hard for them to lose weight. Bullying them doesn't help. It just makes them feel bad."

Quietly, I closed the door and followed our class upstairs. On the way, I remembered what Nurse Mona had told us about health and fitness.

I wasn't fat, but maybe my body wanted to be healthier, too? To find out, I decided to eat as much veg as I could. I'd practise cooking veg in different ways like boiling, roasting and grilling.

Eating more fruit and veg was a good start, but what about keeping fit? Mum said being fit and healthy felt great! I wanted to feel great too!

To be fit and healthy, I decided to try new

activities like dancing and cycling. It would be so much fun!

Wait a minute, I thought. If sports and activities keep people fit and healthy, why is Shelly fat?

Because she stopped eating. It made her so hungry that when she ate something, she ate WAY too much. Eating too much made her fat. That's what I thought. I could've been wrong…

Someday, Shelly would figure out the reason why she was so fat. Then she'd decide whether to stay fat or be slim.

That's exactly what my mum did.

Mum was a fat kid and got fit. She never stopped eating or anything dangerous like that. She ate more veg, ate less junk food, and exercised. If Mum could do it, Shelly could too.

Shelly's going to be just fine, I thought to

myself. It was a hard week but helping her was worth it!

It felt good solving another case. I was so proud of myself. I couldn't wait to tell my parents what I'd done!

But – there's always a BIG but, isn't there? – I knew my secret boss wouldn't be very happy with me. It didn't matter how many teachers gave me a pat on the back. It didn't matter how many students thanked me for helping Shelly. It didn't matter if I'd brought our WHOLE school together without any fussing or fighting.

None of that mattered because I'd messed up my first four big cases. This case had been my last chance, but I got it wrong too. That made my case-solving record look pretty bad.

If police officers have a bad record, they're in serious trouble. A bad police record stays with you for a long time, just like a naughty student record.

"Are you all right, Mya?" Libby asked quietly. "You don't look so good…"

"I'm fine," I said. "Everything's going to be okay."

But I wasn't fine.

And things wouldn't be okay.

I imagined my secret boss shouting at me. She'd say everything I'd done wrong since Monday. She might even take my badge away and kick me off the Children's Police Force.

When I got to my desk, I slipped my hand into my pocket and clutched my badge. It was cold and hard, just like my boss. I didn't want to let go. I wanted to hold on and enjoy it for the last time.

One hour later, my worst fear would come true. My police badge would be taken away from me. I would never see it again…

Chapter 29

In class, everyone was talking about Shelly. It felt like she was a new girl. I couldn't wait to see all the friends she'd make. I wanted to be her friend, too. Shelly, Libby, Jamar, Ricky, Jimmy and me. The best team in the world. No one could stop us!

No one except for...

"Mya," Libby whispered when Mrs Cherry wasn't looking. "The boss wants to see you."

It was time to report the case to my secret boss. She was waiting in the girls' toilets.

"What if she takes my badge away?" I whispered.

"Don't worry, Mya," Libby said. "It'll be okay. You'll see."

I finished my work before putting my hand up. Mrs Cherry let me go to the toilet.

I was sad when I walked to the bathroom. I knew the Children's Police Force might take my badge away. Then I wouldn't be a police officer anymore.

I'd still have my job as a student, but you can't be a student forever. I wanted to be a police officer *forever*, but now my dream was over.

When I reached the girls' toilets, I took a deep breath before going inside.

My secret boss was already there. As usual, she was hiding in a locked toilet stall. I went into the next stall and locked myself in.

She didn't say anything.

My mouth opened but no words came out. I stood there in silence with a thousand thoughts rushing through my head.

My police job is over, I thought. I'll miss solving cases, chasing bad guys and polishing my badge.

I clutched my police badge, enjoying how cold it felt against my skin. I slid my fingers down the badge number: 180289. It didn't matter who took my badge. That number would always be mine.

I won't be Detective Inspector Mya Dove anymore, I thought. Now I'll just be Mya…

"What's wrong with just being Mya?" my mum would say. "Being a police officer is one way to help people. There are *many* other ways to make a positive difference!"

That was true!

Mum helped people as a nurse. When her patients got better, they went home to their family and friends.

Dad helped people as a mechanic. If he didn't fix their cars, they'd be stuck on the motorway in the cold and rain.

Mrs Cherry helped people as a teacher. She taught us to read books, write essays and pass tough exams. Those skills would help us for the rest of our lives.

Mum, Dad and Mrs Cherry all showed that I didn't have to be a police officer to help people. I could still help people with a different job as long as I remembered to be a good person.

A good person knows that doing the right thing is *always* more important than a reward. A good police officer knows that too.

My police job was very important to me, but it would NEVER be more important than my school. My school needed me to solve cases and make things right. Yes, I'd made mistakes. Yes, I'd been wrong a lot. But I kept trying to do my best. Kept fighting the bad guys. Kept being a good person. No matter what happened, I never let being wrong stop me from solving a case.

Besides, being wrong wasn't so bad. My last five cases taught me so much because I'd made mistakes.

On my first case, I learned that quiet people could be scared of talking. Not talking to anyone didn't mean they were mean.

On my second case, I learned that nothing and no one lasts forever. One day we'll all be gone, and that's okay.

On my third case, I learned that some people have very special ears. They hear sounds that no one else can.

On my fourth case, I learned that parents can argue just like kids. It doesn't mean they don't love each other anymore.

This week I learned that we should be nice to fat people, not mean. Being picked on makes them do dangerous things, like not eating food or eating way too much.

I'd learned so much over the past few months. More than any police officer I knew. My boss could take away my badge, but she couldn't take away what I'd learned from each case.

So, no matter what happened next, I was going to be all right. If I went back to being just Mya, that was just fine with me.

My boss stomped three times.

I stomped twice.

She stomped once.

"What's the password?" she asked.

"Children's Police Force."

"Is that Detective Inspector Mya Dove?"

"Yes, I'm here," I said. "You wanted to talk?"

"Did you prove Shelly Walters stole ten burgers from the kitchen?"

"No, because she didn't."

"Detective Inspector, you had orders to prove she stole those burgers!"

I took out the letter she'd sent me on Monday. I read it again, and one more time just to be sure. Then I dropped it on the floor so she could read it.

"You told me to find proof that Shelly was eating too much. Well, I didn't find proof of that because she DOESN'T eat too much. Actually, she wasn't eating at all. Would you like to know why?"

"Not really."

"I'll tell you anyway," I said. "She wasn't eating because mean people like YOU told lies about her. You blamed her for eating all the food just because she's fat."

"How dare you—"

"Sometimes skinny and slim people eat lots of food too. That means anyone could've eaten those burgers. I could've eaten them. Jimmy could've eaten them. YOU could've eaten them!"

"Liar!" My boss stomped her foot. "Take that back!"

"It hurts when people tell lies about you, doesn't it? That's how Shelly feels every time people pick on her for being fat. She knows she's fat. She doesn't need us to tell her."

I smiled. I was about to lose my badge, but so what? Sticking up for Shelly was more important than juicy, sweet, bouncy, green grapes. My mouth was watering just thinking of the grapes I wouldn't be getting.

"Detective Dove, I'm going to remind you who you're talking to!" She stomped her foot again. "You can't talk to me like that!"

I stepped out of my toilet stall and

knocked on her door.

"Come out and say that to my face."

She unlocked the door.

Now I'd finally find out who she was. Was she someone I'd met before, or was she a complete stranger?

When her door opened a crack, my heart started beating so fast. Then she closed the door and locked it.

"Are you coming out?" I asked.

"No, I..."

"Are you okay? Is something wrong?"

"I'm fine," she snapped. "If you didn't prove Shelly Walters stole the burgers, what *did* you prove?"

"I proved that our school will order fewer and fewer burgers until there's none left, and that's okay."

"That's okay?"

"We'll have tasty fruit and vegetables

instead. They taste just as nice as burgers."

"So, you didn't prove Shelly stole the burgers?" she asked.

"Nope because she didn't."

"So, you didn't solve the case?"

"But—"

"Silence," she spat. "I need to think…"

How long is she going to take? I thought. Will I ever get back to class?

"Detective Inspector, you failed to do as I asked. Again."

"I know."

"Place your police badge on the floor."

"Can we talk about this first?"

"Place your police badge on the floor."

"But—"

"Do it now, Detective! Badge. Floor. Now!"

I didn't want her to hear me cry, but I couldn't help it. This was the worst day of my life!

With tears streaming down my cheeks, I put my badge on the floor and stepped away.

"Turn around," she ordered. "Go back into your toilet stall and lock the door."

I returned to the toilet stall. My nose was full of snot and I hated it. I grabbed some toilet tissue and blew my nose before locking the door.

My boss unlocked her door and walked out. She stopped outside my door, where I could see her black, leather shoes. They were shiny and perfectly clean.

She dropped a plastic shopping bag on the floor and kicked it under my door. The bag slid across the floor and stopped at my feet.

"What's that?" I asked.

"Open it," she said. "And stop crying like that. It's REALLY annoying and VERY unprofessional! Police officers don't go around crying like that."

Police officers? But I wasn't a police officer anymore. She'd taken my badge!

I grabbed the bag and tore it open. Inside was a shoebox. It had that weird new shoe smell.

"You bought me new shoes?"

"If you need new shoes, ask your mum and dad," she said. "I've wasted enough time here. I've got classwork to do and other officers to see. Just hurry up and open the box!"

What was inside the shoebox? It couldn't be a present. Mean people like my boss didn't buy presents. What else could it be? There was only one way to find out. So, I opened the shoebox and peered inside…

Chapter 30

I couldn't believe it! When I opened the shoebox, inside was a brand-new, metal police badge. It wasn't anything like my old plastic one.

My old badge was as light as paper. My new badge was heavy, just like a real police badge.

My old badge used to be gold, but it faded because I used it so much. My new badge was shiny and silver like real police badges.

Carved into my brand-new badge was CHILDREN'S POLICE FORCE. Below it was DETECTIVE INSPECTOR. Under that was 180289, my badge number.

This badge is *amazing*, I thought. What else did she buy me?

The biggest box of grapes I'd ever seen! I started eating them right there in the toilet, which is pretty disgusting I know. I didn't care at the time. I wanted them really badly. I should've washed them first, and washed my hands too, but like I said, I didn't care at the time.

Yum, yum, yum. The grapes were so tasty, so sweet. Each one burst in my mouth, letting loose all the juicy bits inside. I gobbled down a few more before stopping myself. I couldn't eat too many or they'd make me poo a lot.

That's TWO amazing gifts, I thought. What else did she bring?

Below the box of grapes was a folded piece of paper. I opened it and read each word aloud:

Dear Mya,

I hope you enjoy your grapes and the new badge. You deserve them for doing such a great job. I heard your speech and it made me very happy to know I work with you.

Most officers would've been mean to Shelly because everyone else was. But you aren't like most officers.
You are special, and I hope you always stay that way.

I popped another grape in my mouth, promising myself it was the last one.

I kept reading the note:

I know I'm hard on you, but that's only because I know you have what it takes to be the second best police officer at school.

I'm the best, of course.

If you keep working hard, you'll do great things. Keep being a good person too. I don't have to tell you how important that is.

Speak to you on Monday.

Do NOT be late!

Kind Regards,
Your Boss

I couldn't believe it. My boss believed in me. She thought I could be the second best police officer in school.

Actually, I was going to be the *first* best police officer, but she didn't need to know that. What she needed to know was that I appreciated my rewards. I'd waited so long to get those grapes!

"Boss, thank you very much," I said, unlocking the door. "This means a lot to me..."

But she'd gone.

I opened the bathroom door and looked up and down the corridor. I could hear the pitter patter of feet running away, but where was the sound coming from?

Too late. My boss was long gone. Besides, I was very late for class. Finding out who my boss was had to wait. Right now, I needed a good excuse for being in the toilet for so long! Oh well. I just had to live with everyone thinking I'd done a poo.

"See you later, Boss." I ate one last grape. And then two more. "I'll speak to you on Monday..."

CASE CLOSED

Dear Reader

Hello, I hope you enjoyed my book. You can email me at contact@zuniblue.com. I'd love to hear from you!

I'd really appreciate it if you left a book review saying whether you loved it, hated it, or thought it was just okay. It doesn't have to be a long review. Thank you very much!

Keep reading to get your 100 free gifts…

About the Author

Zuni Blue lives in London, England with her parents. She's been writing non-fiction and fiction since she was a kid.

She loves telling stories that show how diverse the world is. Her characters are different races, genders, heights, weights and live with various disabilities and abilities. In Zuni's books, every child is special!

Solve More Cases

Would you like to read another case file?

Mya doesn't share her cases with just anyone, but she knows she can trust you.

Keep reading for more top secret cases she's solved…

The Mean Girl Who Never Speaks

There's a new girl at school. She never speaks, never smiles and never plays with other kids. Does that mean she's mean? Maybe. Maybe not...

To solve the mystery, Detective Dove must face a suspicious teacher, the school bully, and the meanest boss in the world...

The School Pet Who Went Missing

Mya's school has a brand new pet. It's cute, cuddly and loves everyone. Unfortunately, it's gone missing! Did it run away? Or was it stolen?

To solve the mystery, Detective Dove must face her bossy headmaster, a mean prefect, and a sneaky teacher with a dark secret...

The New Boy Who Hears Buzzing

The new boy's ears are buzzing. He must've been bugged, but who did it? Was it a student? A teacher? Or some bad guys?

To solve the mystery, Detective Dove must face the detention kids, a crafty inspector, and some naughty officers at the police station...

The Parents With A Sleepover Secret

Mya has to stay at her enemy Angel's house. Angel is forcing her to solve a tough case. If the case isn't solved, Mya will be kicked off the Children's Police Force!

To solve the mystery, Detective Dove must face an angry poodle, a scary garage, and the meanest girl in the universe...

Dedications

This book is dedicated to anyone who struggles with their weight. It's tough, but being fit and healthy is worth all the hard work.

Thank you to my family and friends. I appreciate all the love and support you have given me. I couldn't have done this without you.

An extra special thank you to every reader who's emailed me. I love hearing from you!

100 Free Gifts For You

There are 100 FREE printables waiting for you!

Certificates, bookmarks, wallpapers and more! You can choose your favourite colour: red, yellow, pink, green, orange, purple or blue.

You don't need money or an email address. Check out www.zuniblue.com to print your free gifts today.

Made in the USA
Middletown, DE
17 July 2020